Schooling Around

ALSO BY ANDY GRIFFITHS

Just Annoying!

Just Joking!

Just Stupid!

Just Wacky!

Just Disgusting!

Just Shocking!

The Day My Butt Went Psycho!

Zombie Butts from Uranus!

Butt Wars: The Final Conflict

What Buttosaur Is That?

Schooling Around: Treasure Fever!

Schooling Around

ANDY GRIFFITHS

SCHOLASTIC INC.
New York Toronto London Auckland Sydney
Mexico City New Delhi Hong Kong Buenos Aires

ISBN-13: 978-0-439-92618-8
ISBN-10: 0-439-92618-1

12 11 10 9 8 7 6 5 4 3 2 9 10 11 12 13/0

Printed in the U.S.A. 40

First printing, November 2008

For Judi, Lindsay, Kim, Ajax, and Mad Dog

Chapter 1

Once upon a time

Once upon a time there was — and still is — a school called Northwest Southeast Central School.

Northwest Southeast Central School is located to the southeast of a town called Northwest, which is located to the northwest of Central City.

You don't need to know where Central City is, because it's not important. What *is* important is the school. In this school, there is a classroom. And in that classroom, there is a fifth grade class. Most important of all, in that fifth grade class there is a student named Henry McThrottle who likes to tell stories.

That's where I come in.

I'm Henry McThrottle . . . and this is my latest story.

Chapter 2

The beginning

It all began one morning when I walked through the front gate of Northwest Southeast Central School, across the school yard, up the steps, and through the door of classroom 5B.

I was slightly late, and class had already started.

Not that you would have known it.

Mr. Brainfright, our teacher, was hanging by his toes from one of the ceiling rafters.

His arms were crossed and his face was bright red.

Now, normally, if you walked into a classroom and your teacher was hanging by his toes from the ceiling, you might be a little alarmed. You might ask him if he was all right, or try to help him down, or at the very least, report the situation to another teacher.

But I didn't do any of these things. You see, Mr. Brainfright wasn't a normal teacher. You only had to look at the way he was dressed to tell that. With his purple jacket, orange shirt, and green pants, he looked — and acted — like no other teacher at Northwest Southeast Central School — a fact for which we were *very* grateful. School had been a lot more interesting since he'd taken over from our old teacher, Mrs. Chalkboard.

Today, Mr. Brainfright greeted me with a big smile.

"Good morning, Henry!" he said. "I'm just demonstrating how bats sleep!"

"I've always wondered about that!" I said.

"Well, now you know," said Mr. Brainfright, dismounting with a somersault and landing on his feet. "Any questions, class?"

Fiona McBrain put up her hand.

"Yes, Fiona?" Mr. Brainfright said.

"Will we be tested on this?" she asked.

"Certainly not!" said Mr. Brainfright. "Any other questions?"

"Don't bats sleep in coffins?" Clive Durkin asked.

"That's vampires, Clive!" my friend Jack Japes shouted out, laughing. "Don't you know *anything*?"

Clive narrowed his eyes. "I'm going to tell my brother you said that!" he threatened.

"What?" said Jack. "That bats don't sleep in coffins? He doesn't know, either?"

"No," said Clive. "That you said that I don't know anything."

"No, I didn't!" Jack shot back. He always had an answer to everything. "I just said that vampires, not bats, sleep in coffins!"

"Can you stop talking about bats and vampires?" said my friend Jenny Friendly. "Newton's getting scared."

Jenny was right. Our friend Newton Hooton's eyes were wide as he clutched his lucky rabbit's foot and shook visibly.

"You don't have to be scared of bats, Newton," said Mr. Brainfright. "Or vampires, for that matter."

"Yes, he does," said Jenny. "Newton's scared of everything."

This was true. Newton was scared of everything. He was even scared of being scared. That's how scared he was.

"Oh, yes," said Mr. Brainfright. "Sorry, I forgot."

"Can we do math now?" Fiona asked.

The rest of the class groaned.

"Certainly not!" said Mr. Brainfright.

The class cheered. Everybody, that is, except Fiona.

"But it's Monday morning!" said Fiona. "We always study math on Monday morning!"

"Correction," said Mr. Brainfright. "You always *used* to study math on Monday morning. But today I've got something *much* more important to teach you!"

"What could be more important than math?" said Fiona.

"Magic tricks!" said Mr. Brainfright.

The class cheered again.

"I *love* magic tricks!" said Jack.

"Me too!" boomed Gretel Armstrong. She had a very powerful voice. She also had very strong arms. In fact, she was the strongest girl in the school.

"Me three!" I said.

"Excellent!" said Mr. Brainfright, beaming as he produced a long black magic wand from inside his purple jacket. "I thought we'd start with the vanishing pencil trick. Knowing how to make a pencil vanish is a very important life skill."

I didn't know how true his words were then. But I do now.

Chapter 3

Mr. Brainfright's important lesson no. 1

Knowing how to make a pencil vanish is a very important life skill.

Chapter 4

Magic

We all leaned forward to watch Mr. Brainfright make a pencil vanish.

"The most important thing to know about making a pencil vanish," he said, frowning and patting his coat pockets, "is to make sure you have a pencil *to* vanish. I seem to have vanished all of mine. Does anybody have a pencil that I could borrow?"

"Will we get it back?" asked David Worthy, our class president.

"I hope so," said Mr. Brainfright. "But I can't absolutely guarantee it, of course. I'm going to be using a very powerful spell."

"You can have mine!" I said, opening my pencil case and pulling out the pencil that Mr. Greenbeard, our school principal, had given me as a reward for finding his buried treasure. It had rainbow stripes and a little white eraser in the shape of a skull. The truth was, I didn't like it very much, but I couldn't say why. Maybe it had something to do with the way the eyes of the skull eraser seemed to stare at me.

"Thank you, Henry," said Mr. Brainfright, taking the pencil from my hand. "Everybody ready?"

We all nodded.

Fiona was scribbling notes.

Newton was looking scared.

Mr. Brainfright tapped the pencil with his wand. "Abracadabra," he said. "Make this pencil disappear!" Then he tapped the pencil again with his wand and, I swear, it completely disappeared.

"Voilà!" said Mr. Brainfright, looking as surprised as everybody else.

We all burst into applause.

"That's how you make a pencil vanish!" he said proudly.

"Can you make it come back again?" asked Clive.

"But of course!" said Mr. Brainfright. "Well, I think I can. Stand back, everyone." He raised his wand. "Abracadabra, make the pencil reappear!"

He tapped the wand on the table. Once, twice, a third time, and then . . . *KAPOW!* Pencil shavings exploded out of the end of Mr. Brainfright's wand, directly into his face!

Pencil dust filled the air.

Some of the students who sat in the front row were coughing and gasping for breath, but no one was coughing or gasping more than Mr. Brainfright. His face was turning bright red again, only this time it was brighter and redder than when he'd been hanging upside down. He clutched his throat with both hands, staggered backward across the classroom, and then . . . fell out the window.

We all stared at one another in shock.

Then, thinking that it was all part of the show, the class burst into applause again.

All except me.

I knew something was wrong.

I rushed to the window and looked down.

Mr. Brainfright was lying on his back. Still clutching his throat. Still choking.

I didn't hesitate.

I jumped out the window and landed in the flower bed next to him.

Fortunately, the flower bed was nice and soft, as it had recently been dug up.

For once I didn't have to worry about Mr. Spade, the gardener, getting mad. Mr. Spade was on stress leave after having to fill in all the holes that had been created a few weeks ago when the whole school had been looking for buried treasure.

But even if I didn't have to worry about Mr. Spade, I *did* have to worry about Mr. Brainfright.

He was choking to death!

He stared at me, his eyes pleading for help.

Luckily, just the week before, he'd taught us the Heimlich maneuver, guaranteed to dislodge foreign material from throats.

Without thinking, I jumped up, pulled Mr. Brainfright up from behind, and gave him a violent hug.

He coughed loudly, and then, incredibly, my pencil — now whole again — flew out of his mouth!

There was another round of applause.

I looked up to see everyone from 5B hanging out the window, giving Mr. Brainfright's amazing trick an ovation.

Mr. Brainfright was frowning. "I think they think I did it on purpose," he said, "but I didn't. That wasn't supposed to happen!"

But, as we were soon to find out, what Mr. Brainfright or anybody else wanted to happen didn't matter to this pencil. This pencil had a mind of its own.

Chapter 5

Here comes Fred!

At lunchtime, Jack, Jenny, Gretel, Newton, and I were sitting underneath the trees next to the basketball court.

Jack was picking pickles out of his sandwich and flicking them onto the grass.

Newton's face was white. He was trembling.

"Jack," said Jenny, "can you not do that? You're scaring Newton."

"Huh?" said Jack. "How?"

"He's scared of pickles," Jenny reminded him.

Newton nodded.

"Sorry, Newton," said Jack, closing his sandwich. "I don't like them much, either."

My sandwich was sitting beside me, but I didn't feel like eating. I was still a bit shaken by the incident with Mr. Brainfright.

I took the pencil out of my pocket and examined it carefully.

"I'll tell you what I don't like," I said. "I don't like this pencil. There's something strange about it. Something . . . I don't know . . . *wrong*. It scares me."

Jack laughed. "What a brave pair you are. Newton's scared of pickles and you're scared of a pencil!"

"You're not so brave yourself, Jack," Gretel pointed out.

"Yes, I am," Jack argued. "I'm not scared of *anything*."

Gretel laughed. "Yeah, right."

"Name one thing!" Jack dared her.

"Fred Durkin!" Gretel replied, referring to Clive's big bully of a brother.

"Fred Durkin?" snorted Jack. "Fred Durkin's about as scary as a pickle! Or a pencil, for that matter."

"Oh, really?" Gretel said.

"Really!" Jack replied.

"Well, you're about to get your chance to prove it." Gretel pointed to the other side of the basketball court. "Because here he comes!"

Chapter 6

Yes means no and no means yes

Gretel was right. Fred Durkin was heading straight for us, followed by Clive, who was running to keep up with him.

The blood drained from Jack's face.

"You want me to handle them?" Gretel asked, rolling up her sleeves.

"No," said Jack, chewing his lip. "I'll be fine."

Fred crossed the basketball court.

As he did so, a ball hit him in the head.

I expected him to turn around and kill the poor kid who threw it.

But he didn't.

He didn't even blink.

He just kept walking until he was standing right in front of Jack.

"That's him there, Fred," said Clive, pointing at Jack.

"I see him," said Fred.

"Is there a problem?" said Jack politely.

"Yes, there's a problem," Fred replied. "There's a *big* problem. You disrespected my brother, Japes."

"No, I didn't," said Jack.

"Yes, you did," said Fred. "He said you called him dumb."

"I didn't!"

"Well, he says that you said that he didn't know anything. So, as far as I'm concerned, that's as good as calling him dumb."

"I didn't *say* he didn't know anything," said Jack. "I *asked* him if he didn't. That's all."

"Same thing!" said Clive.

"No, it's not," Jack protested. "That's how dumb you are —" Jack suddenly realized what he'd just said. "Oops."

Fred stared at him for a long time without saying anything.

We all held our breath.

Jack chewed his lip some more.

Then Fred smiled and shook his head. "You know what, Japes?" he said. "Lucky for you I'm in a good mood today. I'm going to give you the benefit of the doubt. In fact, I'm in such a good mood, I'm going to play a little game with you. It's called 'Yes Means No and No Means Yes.' Do you want to play?"

"No," said Jack. "Thanks, but . . ."

"Great!" said Fred, "so you want to play!"

"No. I said no!"

"But no means yes!" said Fred. "That's how we play the game — I ask you a question, and you have to answer yes or no. Okay? Now, are you ready? First question . . . hmm, let me see. Do you want me to punch you?"

Jack opened his eyes wide in alarm. "NO!" he said.

"So you want me to punch you?" said Fred.

"No!" said Jack.

"No means yes and yes means no," Fred reminded him, "so what I'm hearing is that you want me to punch you!"

Clive sniggered.

"No!" said Jack. "I mean yes!"

"Yes, you *do* want me to punch you, or yes, you *don't* want me to punch you?" asked Fred. "Remember, no means yes and yes means no!"

"Yes!" said Jack. *"Yes!"*

Fred looked triumphantly at the group of kids who had formed around us. "Did everybody hear that?" he said, clenching his fist, and drawing it back. "I asked Jack if he wanted me to punch him and he said *yes*!"

"I said *yes*," said Jack, "but yes means no!"

"What are you talking about?" Fred frowned for everyone to see.

"The game!" said Jack. "We're playing the game, remember?"

"I thought you said you didn't want to play," said Fred.

"I did, but . . . I thought you were playing anyway."

Fred smiled. "I *was* playing, but I stopped."

"Then my answer is *no*!" said Jack quickly.

"No, what?"

"No, I don't want you to punch me!"

"No?" said Fred.

"No!" said Jack.

Fred slammed his fist into Jack's arm.

Jack grabbed his arm and fell to the ground. "What did you do that for?"

Fred shrugged innocently. "No means yes and yes means no!"

"But you said you weren't playing that anymore," Jack said.

"I started again," Fred told him.

"That's not fair!"

"I can't help it if you can't keep up."

"It's not fair and you know it," said Jack.

"Are you calling me a cheat?" said Fred.

"No."

"You *are* calling me a cheat?"

"I said *no*," said Jack.

"Yes means no and no means yes," said Fred.

"Then I mean *yes*!" said Jack.

By this time even more kids had gathered around to watch Fred play "Yes Means No and No Means Yes" with Jack.

Fred turned to them now. "You heard that, didn't you?" he said. "He just called me a cheat!"

Some said yes. Some said no. Others just looked confused.

Fred turned to Clive. "I don't believe it!" he said. "He just called me a cheat!"

"That's what I heard," said Clive.

"No, I didn't," said Jack. "Yes means no and no means yes, remember?"

"I'm not playing that anymore," said Fred. "But would you like to play again tomorrow?"

Jack was so confused that he said no, but nodded at the same time.

The crowd laughed.

Poor Jack. I really did feel sorry for him. But, at the same time, I was glad it was him Fred was picking on and not me.

"I'll take that as a yes," said Fred. "See you tomorrow, Japes."

He acted as if he was about to walk off, then turned back and punched Jack on the arm again. "That's for calling me a cheat."

Jack doubled over in pain, clutching his arm.

Fred looked at him scornfully. "Gee, I hate to think how you'd carry on if I hit you *really* hard."

The bell rang for the end of lunch, and the crowd dispersed. Fred and Clive walked away sniggering.

Jack stood up, still rubbing his arm. "Those Durkin

brothers are going to be sorry they messed with me!" he vowed.

"What are you going to do?" said Gretel, chuckling at Jack's bravado. "Let Fred punch you again?"

Jack scowled at her. "You'll see," he promised.

Chapter 7

Jack's cartoon

Jack stomped up the steps and down the corridor toward our classroom.

He was mad.

Madder than I'd ever seen him.

He went straight to his desk, took out a piece of paper, and started drawing.

I knew what this meant.

Jack was going to draw one of his "Fred and Clive" cartoons. Whenever the Durkin brothers annoyed him, he always drew a cartoon of something bad happening to them.

He divided the page into a strip of eight squares and began attacking it with his pencil. He wasn't so much drawing as slashing and stabbing the page.

In fact he was being so violent that he broke his pencil in half.

"Can I borrow your pencil, Henry?" he asked.

Normally, I would have said yes. But I only had one pencil on me . . . and the last time I had lent it out, Mr. Brainfright had ended up flying out the window.

"I don't know," I said. "I don't think it's a good idea. You seem, well, a little *agitated.*"

"I'll get a lot more agitated if you don't lend me your pencil," said Jack, his eyes flashing angrily. "I share all my stuff with you, don't I?"

"Yeah, I guess so," I said, reluctantly getting the pencil out from my pencil case and giving it to him. "Just . . . you know . . . be careful."

Jack nodded. "Okay, Henry," he said. "I won't break this one. I promise."

"That's not what I meant," I said.

"What did you mean?"

"I don't really know."

Jack shrugged and went back to his cartoon.

The skull eraser seemed to grin wider than ever as he worked.

Clive entered the classroom. "Who's the dumb one now, Jack?" he said as he passed our desks. "You don't even know the difference between no and yes."

Jack ignored Clive and kept drawing.

Clive stopped. "I thought your arm would have been too sore to draw!"

"No, it's fine," Jack said, hunching over his drawing so Clive couldn't see it. "Takes more than a girl's punch to hurt me."

"Hey!" yelled Gretel. "I heard that."

"So did I," said Clive. "And I'm going to tell my brother."

"Don't you ever get sick of running to your brother and telling him what everybody said?"

"No," said Clive. "And I'm going to tell him you said that, too!"

Jack didn't say anything.

In fact, Jack didn't say anything for the rest of the afternoon.

Not even when Clive started flicking chewed-up bits of paper at the back of his neck.

Not even when Penny and Gina, the horse-crazy twins in our class, went for a canter around the room on their imaginary horses and bumped into his desk, knocking his cartoon to the floor.

Instead of getting mad, Jack just picked up his paper, placed it back on his desk, and kept drawing.

I'd never seen him so engrossed.

He drew all through our free reading period and it was only when the bell rang that he looked up, blinking.

He picked up his cartoon, stood up, and walked over to my desk.

"Wow!" he said. "That's some pencil, Henry!"

"Really?" I said. "Why?"

"Well, it's going to sound a bit weird," said Jack, "but it was like the pencil was doing all the work. Check it out!"

Jack passed the cartoon to me.

It was called "Flying with Fred and Clive."

Chapter 8

Flying with Fred and Clive

- Frame #1: Fred and Clive flying in a plane.
- Frame #2: Smoke coming out of the back of the plane.
- Frame #3: Fred and Clive jumping out of the plane.
- Frame #4: Fred and Clive trying to open their parachutes.
- Frame #5: Fred and Clive panicking as their parachutes fail to open.
- Frame #6: Fred hitting the ground.
- Frame #7: Clive landing on top of Fred.
- Frame #8: The plane crashing on top of Fred and Clive.

Chapter 9

An apology and a threat

"It's incredible, Jack!" I said. "It's the best drawing you've ever done!"

I wasn't just saying it to be nice, either. I meant it. It was really good. Something about the detail made the pictures look almost real.

"Thanks," said Jack. "But I can't take all the credit. This pencil is great!"

"That's a cool cartoon, Jack," said Gretel, who, along with Jenny and Newton, had come up behind us. "Serves them both right! And Jack?"

"Yes?"

"I'm sorry for teasing you at lunch."

"Are you really sorry or are you just scared that Jack will draw a cartoon of you?" I teased.

"Both!" said Gretel, laughing.

"It's *really* good, Jack," said Jenny, "but I can't help feeling a little bit sorry for Fred and Clive."

"Feel sorry for them?" said Jack. "How about feeling sorry for me? I'm the one who got my arm punched . . . twice!"

"I know," said Jenny, pointing at the final frame of the cartoon. "But all the same . . . that must hurt!"

"So did getting punched on the arm!" Jack protested.

"What's wrong, Newton?" Gretel asked.

We looked at Newton. His face was white.

He was trying to talk, but no words were coming out.

"Is it the cartoon?" Jenny asked gently. "Are you scared of Jack's cartoon?"

Newton shook his head. "What if . . ." he said, taking a deep breath. "What if Fred and Clive see it?"

"That won't happen," said Jack.

"Won't it?"

We turned around.

Clive was standing right behind Jack. He was shaking his head. "My brother's definitely not going to like this," he said. "He's not going to like this at all!"

"He doesn't have to know," said Jack.

"Oh, yes he does," said Clive, turning and heading off down the corridor. "As soon as possible!"

"You know what your problem is, Clive?" Jack shouted after him. "You need to get a life!"

Clive turned back and smiled. "I've got one," he said. "It's you who's going to need a life when Fred finds out about this!"

Jack gulped. He looked even more frightened than Newton, if that was possible.

Suddenly, “Flying with Fred and Clive” didn’t seem quite as funny as it had a few minutes earlier.

And it was about to get even unfunnier.

In fact, none of us had any idea just *how* unfunny things were about to get.

Chapter 10

Bad news

The next morning, Mr. Brainfright called the class to order.

"I'm afraid I've got some bad news," he said.

"Oh, no," said Gretel. "You're not leaving, are you?"

"No, nothing like that," Mr. Brainfright assured her.

"Our next vacation has been canceled?" I suggested.

"No," said Mr. Brainfright. "Not quite *that* bad."

"The vacation has been *extended*?" Fiona gasped.

"What would be bad about that?" asked Mr. Brainfright.

"I *love* school!" said Fiona. "There's so much to learn and so little time. The more school, the better, as far as I'm concerned."

"Ah, yes," said Mr. Brainfright, "I couldn't agree more. But that's not the bad news. The bad news is that I've had word that Clive and his brother, Fred, are in the hospital. They are both in a very serious condition and may not return to school for quite some time. . . ."

"What happened?" said Jenny, looking worried.

"Well," said Mr. Brainfright, "apparently they were on their garage roof trying to launch a model airplane. Fred fell off the roof and then Clive did, too . . . and landed right on top of Fred! And then, to add insult to injury, their plane rolled off the roof and crashed on top of Clive."

As he was telling us this, some kids started giggling.

"Come now, children," said Mr. Brainfright. "It's not funny . . . not funny at all!"

He was right. It wasn't funny.

Newton, Gretel, Jenny, Jack, and I stared at one another in open-mouthed astonishment.

It was just like Jack's cartoon! Well, give or take a few small details, but the result was the same.

I looked out the window and noticed a cloud pass in front of the sun. A sudden wind blew autumn leaves off a tree in a wild flurry.

I opened my pencil case and looked at the pencil.

The skull winked at me.

Chapter 11

Nice things

We went straight from morning roll call to the art room.

Mrs. Rainbow, the art teacher, gave us all a big smile as we came in.

Mrs. Rainbow loved art and encouraged us to explore and express ourselves in whatever way we felt like. The only way she didn't like us expressing ourselves was in the form of clay-fights, paint-fights, or running with scissors.

Apart from that, it was pretty much anything goes.

Jenny, Gretel, Newton, Jack, and I sat at the collage table in the back of the room, but we weren't doing any collage. All we could think about was what had happened to Fred and Clive.

"It's just like your cartoon, Jack!" said Jenny.

"No, it's not," Jack replied. "It's nothing like it! In my cartoon they were flying in an airplane and then had engine trouble and had to bail out and their parachutes failed to open!"

"And then?" said Jenny.

Jack made a face. "Hmmm . . . let me see. Well, I think Fred hit the ground and then Clive fell on top of him and the airplane crashed on top of them both. . . ."

"Notice any similarities?" Jenny asked.

"None at all," said Jack, stubborn as always. "Well . . . maybe a couple. What are you trying to say? That my cartoon *caused* their accident?"

"Way to go, Jack!" said Gretel. "They sure had it coming!"

"It's not funny," said Jenny.

"I didn't say it *was* funny," said Jack. "But it's not my fault! It's never happened before with any of my cartoons. It's just a coincidence!"

"No," I said, "it's too close for coincidence. It's the pencil. There's something weird, something dangerous about that pencil!"

"Don't be stupid, Henry," said Jack. "It's a really, really good pencil."

"Not true!" I said. "Remember how it made Mr. Brainfright fall out the window and almost choke to death?"

"That wasn't the pencil's fault!" said Jack, shaking his head. "It's not the first time Mr. Brainfright's fallen out the window. He fell out twice in one day once.

Remember? Or are you conveniently forgetting that fact?"

"No," I said. "But you're conveniently forgetting the fact that what you drew about Fred and Clive came true!"

"What are you saying?" said Jack. "That the pencil is cursed? Is that what you're trying to tell me?"

"I don't know," I said. "Maybe."

"That's ridiculous," said Jack.

"Maybe," I told him. "But maybe not. I once read a story about a writer who had this typewriter and whatever stories he wrote on the typewriter came true. He wrote a story about a really powerful monster that couldn't be destroyed by bullets or bombs, and then a real monster just like the one he described started attacking the city. In the end the only way to destroy the monster and save the city was to destroy the typewriter that he'd written the story on."

By now, Newton's eyes were practically popping out of his face in terror.

"It's okay, Newton," Jenny said, patting his arm. "It's just a story."

"But it *could* happen," I said.

"Are you going to destroy the pencil?" Jack said. "Because I won't let you. I've never drawn as well as I did with that pencil. *It's the best pencil ever!*"

"How are you all doing?" asked Mrs. Rainbow, coming up to the collage table. "Have you started yet?"

"Not exactly, Mrs. Rainbow," Jenny answered.

"Having trouble getting ideas?"

"No," said Gretel. "We're just having a discussion . . . about a pencil."

"Anything I can help you with?"

"Yes," I said, looking pointedly at Jack. "What would you do if you had a pencil and you had good reason to believe that whatever you drew with it came true?"

Mrs. Rainbow smiled. "A *magic* pencil?"

"Maybe," I said.

"Well," said Mrs. Rainbow, "if I was lucky enough to have a pencil like that, I think I would only draw nice things with it."

"Nice things," I said. "Of course! That's brilliant! Thanks, Mrs. Rainbow."

"Pleased to be of service," she said, her attention turning to a loud noise on the other side of the room. Penny had just fallen off the life-size papier-mâché pony she and Gina had been working on for the last few months.

"So we don't have to destroy the pencil?" said Jack, as Mrs. Rainbow quickly moved away to assist Penny.

"We need to do an experiment first," I said.

"But I don't want anybody else to get hurt," said Jenny.

"Don't worry," I assured her, "we won't draw anything bad. This time, like Mrs. Rainbow suggested, we'll draw something nice and see if it comes true. That way we'll know if it's really magic or not!"

Chapter 12

Jenny's picture

Jenny smiled. "You know what?" she said. "I've always wanted a kitten. Can I draw that?"

"Of course you can," I said, giving her the pencil. "I don't see how a kitten could hurt anybody."

Jenny took a piece of paper and began to draw herself holding a really cute kitten. Although Jenny was nowhere near as good at drawing as Jack, her picture had the same special quality that had made Jack's drawing so vivid.

It was a beautiful picture.

So cute and so alive!

You could practically hear the kitten purring.

Chapter 13

Gretel's picture

"That's great, Jenny," said Gretel, reaching for the pencil. "You've given me an idea!"

"What are you going to draw?" I said.

"Something that I've always wanted, too," said Gretel, her eyes shining.

"A kitten?" Newton guessed.

"No," said Gretel. "To beat my dad at arm wrestling. He's the only person I can't beat . . . besides myself, of course."

We nodded.

Gretel was the strongest girl in the school. And not only the strongest girl, but the strongest person. Nobody else in the school could beat her at arm wrestling. Not even Mr. Grunt, the gym teacher, and he had arms as thick as most people's legs.

I could only imagine how thick Gretel's dad's arms must be. Well, I didn't have to imagine for long. Gretel's picture told the whole story.

Chapter 14

Henry's picture

"I'm done," said Gretel, passing the pencil to me. "Your turn, Henry. What do you want?"

What did I want?

That was easy. I wanted to win *The Northwest Chronicle*'s annual short-story competition. This year I'd entered a story called "Treasure Fever." The presentation was to be held that evening in the town square. The winner got a framed certificate and one hundred dollars in prize money.

I'd received a letter telling me that my story was on the shortlist, but I wasn't holding out any real hope of winning the big prize.

There was some tough competition out there this year. I knew both Fiona McBrain and David Worthy had entered, and they were both really good at everything.

I figured a little extra help couldn't hurt.

I held the pencil tightly.

The skull winked.

I shuddered and, despite a bad feeling in my stomach, began to draw.

Chapter 15

Jack's picture

When I'd finished, Jack looked at my drawing and laughed.

"What's so funny?" I said.

"You are," he said. "All of you. Believing that you've got a magic pencil. Next you'll be telling me fairies are real."

"What do you mean?" said Newton, looking alarmed. "Fairies *are* real, aren't they?"

"Of course they are, Newton," said Jenny, patting his shoulder and frowning at Jack. "Of course they are!"

"Nobody said it was *magic,*" I said. "We're just doing a test, that's all. Are you going to be in it?"

"I don't think so," said Jack. "I live in the *real* world."

"What have you got to lose?" I said. "If it doesn't work, you haven't lost anything. If it does work, you can have anything you want."

"I guess you're right," said Jack. "Now that you put it like that . . . a million dollars would be nice."

I handed him the pencil. "Draw it, then," I said.

Jack shrugged. "Okay," he said. "This is me with a million dollars." And he drew a picture of himself with his head sticking out from under a huge pile of money.

X

Chapter 16

The finished pictures

When Jack had finished, he offered the pencil to Newton, but Newton just shook his head.

He was too frightened to wish for anything.

And if we'd known then what we know now, we would have been, too.

In fact, if we'd known then what we know now, we would have ripped those pictures to shreds, set fire to the pieces, and then pounded the ashes into dust and pounded the dust into atoms and the atoms into protons and the protons into quarks, which are the smallest particles of matter that exist and can't hurt anyone, not even a flea.

But we didn't.

None of us had any idea of the forces of chaos that we had just unwittingly unleashed.

Chapter 17

Chase!

We didn't have to wait long.

In fact, Jack hardly had to wait at all.

That lunchtime, as usual, we were all sitting out in the school yard, underneath the trees next to the basketball court.

Jack was picking pickles out of his sandwich and flicking them onto the grass, as usual.

Newton was getting scared, as usual, but before Jenny could ask Jack not to flick pickles like she usually did, we heard a siren in the distance.

"What's that?" Newton asked.

"A police siren!" Jack told him, jumping up and leaning over the fence to look down the road and get a glimpse of the police car.

"Yikes!" said Newton. "I'm scared of police!"

"Don't worry about it!" said Jack. "You haven't done anything wrong, have you?"

"No," said Newton. "But other people might have."

Newton didn't know how true his words were.

The siren was getting louder. It was definitely coming toward us. We all got up and joined Jack at the fence.

A black car was speeding up the road.

"That's strange," said Gretel. "It doesn't *look* like a police car."

"That's because it's *not* a police car," said Jack. "It's a getaway car! The police are chasing it!"

"Oh, dear," said Jenny. "That's dangerous. I sure hope nobody gets hurt!"

As the black car roared past us, one of the doors opened and a large bag was thrown out.

The bag flew through the air, across the road, and over the fence. It hit Jack square in the chest, knocking him onto his back. Then the bag burst open and Jack disappeared underneath a small mountain of hundred-dollar bills.

"Wow!" Newton gasped. "There must be at least a *million* dollars there!"

I thought about the picture Jack had drawn with the pencil.

"You know what, Newton?" I said. "I'd say there's *exactly* one million dollars there."

Jack's picture was identical to the scene in front of us: Jack lying on his back underneath a million dollars worth of cash. The only difference was that I was pretty sure Jack hadn't intended his million dollars to be flung at him from a speeding car.

"Are you all right, Jack?" said Jenny, shaking his shoulder.

Jack opened his eyes. "I think so," he said. "What happened?"

"You're a millionaire!" I said. "Congratulations!"

The sirens were loud now.

There were two police cars.

One car roared past in hot pursuit of the black car.

The other police car pulled up beside us. Two burly officers jumped out, leaped over the fence, and pulled Jack out from under the money and onto his feet.

"You're under arrest," said one of them, clicking handcuffs around his wrists.

"What for?" said Jack, blinking and still dazed.

"For aiding and abetting a bank robbery," said the other officer. "You're in big trouble, kid!"

"But he didn't have anything to do with it!" said Gretel, moving to help Jack. "Take those off him!"

"Step back," commanded the first officer, "or you'll be charged with helping a suspect to resist arrest!"

At that, Newton fell to the ground from the shock of it all.

I felt something in my hand.

It was the pencil. I had no idea how it had gotten there, but there it was. And the eyes on the skull were definitely flashing.

Newton wasn't the only one who was scared.

Jenny knelt down to help him.

"What's wrong with him?" said the second officer, pointing at Newton.

"You're scaring him," said Jenny.

"He should be happy!" said the first officer. "We're the good guys!"

"If you're the good guys, I'd hate to see the bad guys!" said Mr. Brainfright, who had just arrived. "Uncuff that boy this instant!"

"Sorry," said the first officer, "I can't do it. The Northwest Bank was robbed this morning. We have reason to believe that this boy is part of the gang that did it."

"Part of the gang?" said Mr. Brainfright. "Why, that's preposterous!"

"We caught him red-handed with the loot!" said the second officer.

"That boy is no bank robber!" said Mr. Brainfright. "And I should know! His name is Jack Japes. He's in my fifth grade class. He's been at school all morning. The bank robbers obviously discarded some of their stolen loot to distract you and slow you down. You should be chasing them instead of frightening innocent schoolboys."

The officers looked at each other.

"All right, then," said the first officer. "We'll take your word for it."

The second officer uncuffed Jack. "What your teacher is telling us might be true, but we'll be keeping an eye on you all the same, Jack Japes."

They stuffed all the money back into the bag, jumped the fence, and drove away.

"Do you believe that the pencil has magic powers now?" I whispered to Jack.

"No," said Jack. "They took my million dollars away!"

Chapter 18

The Northwest Chronicle

At 6:30 that evening, I was standing in the Northwest town square with a couple of hundred other people waiting for the announcement of the winners of the junior section of *The Northwest Chronicle* short-story competition.

The Northwest brass band was doing its best to keep us entertained despite the cold gusts of wind that were blasting the crowd while we waited for the official ceremony to begin.

Many other students from Northwest Southeast Central School were there. Last year's winner, Fiona McBrain, was waiting at the front of the stage. She was obviously expecting to win again. David Worthy, who won last year's second place, was standing next to her.

I went and stood next to them, feeling a mixture of excitement and dread.

I had a good story and a good chance of winning. But after what had happened to Jack that afternoon, I was nervous.

I didn't trust that pencil.

Especially when I realized that it was in my pocket, despite the fact that I had intended not to bring it.

I pulled it out and looked at it.

The skull was grinning.

I shuddered and shoved it back into my pocket.

At that moment, the mayor arrived. He was a tall man, with a big important-looking gold chain around his neck.

As the band finished, he strode confidently up the steps, followed by the editor of *The Northwest Chronicle* and a few other official-looking people, one of whom was carrying a giant cardboard check.

An official-looking man made a speech.

An official-looking woman made a speech.

The editor made a speech.

Finally, the mayor stood in front of the microphone, holding two envelopes. "It is now my great pleasure to award second place to . . ." He paused to open the envelope. "Fiona McBrain for her story, 'My Grandmother's House.'"

The crowd applauded. Fiona looked shocked as she walked up the stairs to collect her certificate. I don't think she was shocked that she had won. I think she was shocked that she had come in second. Fiona McBrain was not used to coming in second.

"And now," said the Mayor, "without further ado, it is my even greater pleasure to award first place in *The Northwest Chronicle*'s writing competition to . . ." He paused again while he opened the envelope, "Henry McThrottle for his story, 'Treasure Fever.'"

The crowd applauded again.

I walked up the stairs and shook the mayor's hand as he gave me my certificate.

I couldn't believe it. I'd done it. I'd won the writing competition I'd been trying to win ever since I was old enough to write. I stood there basking in the crowd's applause. I could see my mother and father beaming.

"Well done, Henry," said the mayor. "But don't go yet — I think the editor of *The Northwest Chronicle* has a small gift for you."

The crowd laughed.

There was nothing small about the enormous cardboard check that the editor was attempting to carry across the stage, his progress hampered by the strong wind.

He was struggling to hold on to it, and suddenly, the wind ripped it from his grasp and it flew across the stage toward me.

The next thing I knew I was lying on my back, looking up at the sky.

There was blood everywhere.

My neck was stinging.

"Somebody call an ambulance!" yelled the mayor.

Chapter 19

Northwest Central Hospital

I was rushed to the emergency room at Northwest Central Hospital.

As it turned out, I was okay, apart from having what the doctor described as the nastiest paper cut she had ever seen.

The check had nearly cut my head off!

The doctor bandaged it up, told me that I was lucky to still have my head, and discharged me.

I sat in the waiting room while my parents completed the paperwork and was amazed to see Gretel there. Her arm was in a sling.

"Henry!" she said. "What happened to your neck?"

"Oh, just a little accident with an oversize check," I said.

"What?"

"Well, I won the writing competition, but when they were presenting me with the winner's check, the wind blew it out of the editor's hand and it almost chopped off my head. What happened to *you*?"

"I broke my wrist," she said. "My dad and I were arm wrestling. Dad was winning, but then I suddenly felt this huge surge of power. I managed to get my arm back up and then I slammed his down onto the table. That's when I heard the crack, and my wrist started throbbing and swelling up."

"Is your dad all right?" I asked.

"Yes," said Gretel. "Except for being a little upset that I beat him, of course."

I nodded. "I guess we have our answer."

"What do you mean?" she said.

"That pencil is dangerous," I said. "Even when you draw something nice, something bad happens."

"You think the pencil's responsible for our injuries?"

"Look at the evidence," I said. "First it was Fred and Clive who suffered. Then Jack. Now it's you and me. The question isn't whether the pencil is responsible or not: The question is, who will be next?"

We looked at each other.

"Jenny?" said Gretel.

"Yes," I nodded.

"But she drew a kitten," said Gretel. "Kittens aren't dangerous! They're cute!"

"Let's hope so," I said.

Chapter 20

Back in class

The next day at school, I had a big white bandage around my neck.

Gretel had her arm in a sling.

Jenny was very worried about us, although she was okay herself.

Newton was scared that something was going to happen to him, even though he hadn't drawn anything with the the pencil.

Jack was sympathetic, but still refused to believe that our injuries were due to anything more than coincidence.

The first half of the day was relatively uneventful.

Nobody was hit by flying bags of money, giant checks, or people falling off the roof.

Mr. Brainfright didn't even fall out the window.

Not once!

The trouble didn't start until after lunch.

Chapter 21

How to cut a student in half

As we came in from recess, we found Mr. Brainfright standing behind a long black box that was mounted on top of a stainless steel cart. The box was decorated with yellow stars.

Mr. Brainfright was wearing a black cape and had a shiny silver saw in his hand.

"What are you going to do?" said Jack, grinning. "Cut somebody in half?"

"That's exactly what I'm going to do, my boy," said Mr. Brainfright. "Knowing how to cut somebody in half is a very important life skill — though perhaps not as important as knowing how to put him back together. But don't worry, I'll teach you that as well!"

There was a burst of excited chatter. The prospect of watching Mr. Brainfright cut somebody in half certainly beat the prospect of math, or English, or history, or . . . well . . . *anything,* really.

"I need a volunteer," said Mr. Brainfright.

The excited chatter stopped.

The room went completely silent.

Chapter 22

Mr. Brainfright's important lesson no. 2

Knowing how to cut somebody in half is a very important life skill — though perhaps not as important as knowing how to put him back together.

Chapter 23

Jenny volunteers

Mr. Brainfright looked around. "Come now, 5B," he said. "Surely one of you would like to be cut in half? I promise I'll put you back together again. Well, I'll try my best, anyway."

It was not exactly a promise that filled any of us with great confidence or an overwhelming desire to jump into his box, despite the twinkle in his eye.

"What's the matter, 5B?" Mr. Brainfright asked, looking hurt. "Don't you trust me?"

"I'll do it," said Jenny, getting up from her desk. She couldn't stand to see anybody looking sad . . . even if he was just pretending to be sad in order to get somebody to volunteer herself to be cut in half.

"Good for you, Jenny!" said Mr. Brainfright, holding one end of the box open for her. "Just wriggle in here and relax."

Gretel and I looked at each other, alarmed.

Jenny hadn't drawn anybody getting cut in half, but given what had happened to everybody else, we didn't like seeing her taking such an unnecessary risk.

"No," I said, "don't do it!"

"Why not?" said Jenny.

"It's dangerous!"

"No, it's not," said Mr. Brainfright. "Well, maybe just a little, but that's all part of the fun. You can't make an omelet without cracking a few eggs! Are you comfortable, Jenny?"

"Yes," said Jenny. "It's quite relaxing."

"Can you wiggle your legs?"

"I think so," she said, and her feet, which were sticking out the other end of the box, wiggled.

"Excellent!" said Mr. Brainfright. Then he turned to the class. "Now, the first thing you need to know about cutting somebody in half is that you need to make sure your saw is sharp." He touched one of the teeth on his saw. "Ouch! Are you ready, Jenny?"

Jenny nodded enthusiastically.

Mr. Brainfright placed the saw on the top of the box and began to saw.

And saw.

And saw.

And saw.

We were all on the edge of our seats.

Then we were on the edge of the edge of our seats.

Then we were on the edge of the edge of the edge of our seats.

"I'm scared!" Newton cried.

"Don't be," said Jenny. "I'm not scared, and it doesn't hurt a bit!"

Finally, incredibly, Mr. Brainfright sawed right through the box.

Jenny was still smiling.

Even more miraculously, she was still smiling when Mr. Brainfright dramatically pushed the halves of the box apart, sending the top half of her body one way, and her legs — still kicking — the other way.

"Voilà!" said Mr. Brainfright.

"Will we be tested on this?" asked Fiona.

Chapter 24

Some very bad news

Before Mr. Brainfright could answer Fiona, the classroom PA speaker crackled into life.

"Attention, crew," said the voice of Principal Greenbeard, "I have some news of a dire nature to impart. Batten down the hatches. I repeat, *batten down the hatches*."

Now, before I go on, what you should know about Principal Greenbeard is that he loves ships and sailing. And when I say he loves ships and sailing, I mean he *really* loves ships and sailing. In fact, he loves ships and sailing so much that he acts as if the school is one huge ship, that all the teachers and students are sailors, and that he, of course, is the captain.

It's important that you know this, otherwise you might think he is a bit crazy.

Well, obviously, he is a *bit* crazy, but he isn't *all* crazy. He's just crazy about anything to do with ships and sailing.

And when he says *batten down the hatches*, that means trouble.

Principal Greenbeard continued to speak. "Now, I

don't wish to alarm you," he said, "but we've just been notified that a circus lion has escaped and there have been several sightings that indicate the beast is heading in our direction at an alarming rate of knots. I would just like to warn all crew members to stay inside and keep all cabin doors and portholes fully secured. I repeat, batten down all hatches until further notice. Thank you all, and please remember that it's very important that we do not panic."

The announcement finished.

People started panicking.

Some students screamed.

Some students jumped up on their chairs.

Some students screamed *and* jumped up on their chairs.

But nobody screamed louder than Newton. "Aaaaggghhh!" he wailed. "I'm scared of lions!"

"You're not the only one this time," said Gretel. "We're *all* scared of lions!"

"No, you don't understand!" said Newton. "On my top-ten list of things that I'm scared of, lions take up nine places!"

"You have a list?" said Mr. Brainfright.

Newton nodded.

"That you carry around with you?"

"Yes," said Newton, reaching into his pocket and pulling out a crumpled piece of paper and handing it to Mr. Brainfright. "I have it right here."

Chapter 25

Newton's top-ten list of things he is scared of

1. Lions
2. Lions
3. Lions
4. Lions
5. Lions
6. Lions
7. Lions
8. Lions
9. Fred Durkin
10. Lions

Chapter 26

Escaped lion!

Mr. Brainfright handed Newton's list back to him. "Most impressive," he said. "But don't worry about a thing. As long as we don't go outside, we'll be fine."

"Mr. Brainfright," said Gina, "can Penny and I go outside for a minute?"

"No, of course not!" said Mr. Brainfright. "There's a lion on the loose!"

"But that's exactly why we need to go outside!" said Penny. "Our horses are tied up to a tree!"

"I'm afraid not, girls," said Mr. Brainfright, a little gentler now. "It's too risky."

"But they'll get eaten by the lion!" Gina cried.

"Well, that's good, isn't it?" said Jack. "If it eats your horses, then it will be too full to eat any of us!"

Penny and Gina both looked horror-stricken and bolted for the door.

"Stop them!" said Mr. Brainfright.

Gretel, who was close to the door, stood up and blocked the way. "Sorry, girls," she said. "You heard Mr. Brainfright. The horses are going to have to take their chances outside."

"If anything happens to them, we're going to hold you and Mr. Brainfright responsible," said Penny, putting her arm around Gina, who was too upset to speak.

"Now, calm down, everybody," said David, standing up at the front of the class. "We can get through this. We can. But it's important that we don't panic. We all need to lie on the floor and not move a muscle."

Everybody in the class, including Mr. Brainfright, dropped to the ground.

"What about me?" said Jenny.

In all the excitement we'd forgotten about Jenny.

"You're already lying down," said Mr. Brainfright. "You'll be fine."

"Okay," said Jenny, who wasn't smiling quite as much as before.

"All right," said David. "Good work, everybody. If we all stay perfectly still, the lion will assume we're dead and move on."

"Hang on," said Fiona, sitting up. "That's bears. That's how you protect yourself against a bear attack!"

"Oh . . . is it?" said David, looking a little confused. "Maybe you're right. Okay . . . actually, we don't have to lie down but we should all stay very still because lions have very poor eyesight."

Everybody got up on their feet and froze like statues.

"What about me?" said Jenny.

"Just don't move," said Mr. Brainfright. "You'll be fine."

"Okay," said Jenny, who wasn't smiling at all now.

"Just remember, everybody, don't get downwind of the lion," said David, "because they have an extraordinarily well-developed sense of smell, and —"

"That's rhinoceroses," said Fiona, "*not* lions!"

"Really?" said David, frowning.

"Yes, of course!" said Fiona. "*Everybody* knows that!"

"Yeah," said David, blushing. "I was just joking."

"Joking at a time like this?" I said.

"It's important to keep a sense of humor at all times," Mr. Brainfright pointed out.

"Not when you're being ripped apart by a lion, it isn't!" I said.

"No, you're wrong, Henry," said Mr. Brainfright. "That's when a sense of humor is *especially* important!"

Chapter 27

Mr. Brainfright's important lesson no. 3

It's important to keep a sense of humor at all times — *especially* when you're being ripped apart by a lion.

Chapter 28

It's here!

David was practically hyperventilating as he tried to recall the correct method for dealing with lions in the classroom. "Hold on, I remember now," he gasped. "We all need to stomp and the vibrations will scare it away. Lions are a lot more scared of us than we are of them!"

Everybody started stomping loudly on the floor.

"*Stop!*" yelled Fiona. "That's *snakes*! Not lions! *Stop!!!*"

But nobody stopped stomping. They were having too much fun.

"Oh, no!" said Fiona. "Every lion for hundreds of miles around is going to be attracted to our classroom now!"

"Look on the bright side," said Mr. Brainfright.

"What bright side?" Fiona asked.

"We should be fairly safe from snakes!" he said, his eyes twinkling.

"May I remind you that it wasn't a snake that escaped from the circus," said Fiona. "It was a *lion*!"

"*Shush!*" yelled Gretel, her powerful voice cutting through the noise.

Everybody stopped stomping instantly.

"What?" I said.

Gretel was standing on a chair, peering out through the top row of windows that ran along the corridor.

But she didn't answer.

She just screamed.

"*It's here!*" she yelled. "The lion is in the corridor!"

"See what you did?" Fiona said to David.

"Well, I'm sorry!" he said. "But I was just trying to help, you know!"

Suddenly, there was a huge crash against the classroom door.

I caught a glimpse of a huge, angry, slobbering face against the window. And for once it wasn't Mrs. Cross coming to tell Mr. Brainfright to keep the noise down. It was a lion. *The* lion.

"Goodness gracious," exclaimed Mr. Brainfright, "look at it! What a *magnificent* beast! No wonder they call the lion the king of the jungle!"

The lion crashed against the door again. The door shook.

"Quick!" said Gretel, dragging a desk across the floor despite her broken wrist. "Help me barricade the door!"

But it was too late.

Before we could help Gretel, there was another huge crash. The door fell off its hinges. The lion leaped across it and into the room.

"Everybody stay calm!" said David.

The lion roared.

David screamed and jumped out the window.

Chapter 29

Kitty

The lion roared again and moved toward the window as if it was going to follow David . . . but then it stopped, turned, and looked at Jenny's top half.

Jenny was still lying in the magic box, staring in horror at the lion.

"Don't move, Jenny," said Mr. Brainfright.

"I can't!" she said very quietly.

The lion advanced slowly toward her.

We all stared.

Except for Mr. Brainfright, who picked up a chair with one hand, whipped off his belt with the other, and cracked it above his head like a whip.

The lion turned and snarled at him.

Mr. Brainfright waved the chair at the lion and cracked his belt-whip again as if he had been a professional lion tamer before becoming a schoolteacher. And knowing Mr. Brainfright, he probably had.

But despite his skill, the lion wasn't interested in being tamed.

It roared at Mr. Brainfright and then turned back to Jenny.

Then, to everybody's amazement, Newton spoke.

Well, it was more of a squeak really.

But it was very brave of him nonetheless.

"Leave her alone!" he squeaked.

The lion turned toward him.

"Yikes!" said Newton.

Just at that moment the lion opened its massive jaws and roared.

Newton's arm shot up into the air, and his lucky rabbit's foot flew out of his hand and headed straight for the lion's head.

The not-so-lucky-now rabbit's foot went shooting into the lion's open mouth and right down into its throat.

The roar turned into a strangled rasp. The lion started heaving and making a weird coughing noise, just like a cat with a hair ball.

"Somebody *do* something!" said Jenny, who couldn't stand to see anything suffer, even if it was a mad beast that had just considered eating her. "The poor thing is choking!"

"Never fear, Brainfright is here!" said Mr. Brainfright. He put down his chair and belt and leaped to the lion's rescue. With one arm around its neck, Mr. Brainfright held it tight while he reached down into its throat.

He pulled the rabbit's foot out of the lion's mouth. It was covered in lion's spit, but still intact.

"Here you are, Newton," he said, tossing the soggy rabbit's foot across the classroom.

Newton caught it and grinned. "Thanks, Mr. Brainfright," he said.

"No, thank *you*, Newton," said Mr. Brainfright. "That was very quick thinking on your part. If it hadn't been for you, Jenny would have been devoured in front of our very eyes . . . well, her top half at least!"

Newton's grin quickly faded.

"But I wasn't!" said Jenny, quickly. "Thank you, Newton!"

Newton managed a small smile in response.

The lion licked Mr. Brainfright's hand. "Do a lion a favor and it's your friend for life," he said. He patted the lion on the head. "He's just like a big kitten, really. And he's even got a collar with a little bell and a name tag on it. Let's see what he's called."

Mr. Brainfright flipped the name tag around. "How fitting!" he said. "His name is *Kitty*!"

At the sound of his name, the lion purred with pleasure and nudged Mr. Brainfright affectionately.

But at the sound of his name my stomach dropped.

Jenny had used the pencil to draw herself getting a kitten.

She'd got a "kitten" all right . . . and it had almost killed her.

That pencil was not only dangerous, but it had a sick sense of humor as well.

"I'd like to get out of the box now," said Jenny. "Can you put me back together again?"

"Of course!" said Mr. Brainfright. "I'll just let the circus know we've found their lion and be right with you!"

Chapter 30

Mr. Brainfright's guide to protecting yourself against lions in the classroom

Reading the preceding chapter may have gotten you worried about lions getting into your classroom. Relax — it's probably not going to happen.

Nevertheless, after our lion attack Mr. Brainfright came up with this handy guide to protecting yourself against lions.

We put it up in our classroom, and I think it would be a good idea if you were to photocopy it and put it up in yours.

As Jenny's mother says, it's better to be safe than sorry.

1. Make sure the hallway is well lit so that you could see a lion if one were present.
2. Remove corridor clutter to eliminate hiding places for lions. Make it difficult for lions to approach unseen.
3. Make lots of noise if you come and go during dusk to dawn, the time lions are active.

4. Keep the classroom door closed. Don't let a lion into your classroom under any circumstances, no matter how nicely it asks.
5. When you go outside your classroom, go in groups and make plenty of noise to reduce your chances of surprising a lion. A sturdy walking stick is a good idea, since it can be used to ward off a lion. Make sure you stay close together and within sight of one another at all times.
6. Don't approach a lion, especially one that is feeding or with cubs. Most lions will try to avoid a confrontation. Give them a way to escape.
7. Stay calm when a lion breaks into your classroom. Talk calmly yet firmly to it and move slowly.
8. Stop or back away slowly, if you can do so safely. Running may stimulate a lion's instinct to chase and attack. Face the lion and stand upright.
9. Do what you can to appear larger. Raise your arms and open your jacket if you are wearing one.
10. If the lion behaves aggressively, throw books or pencil cases without crouching down or turning your back. Wave your arms slowly and speak firmly. Your goal is to convince the lion that you are not prey and that you may be a danger to it.

11. Fight back if a lion attacks you. Lions have been driven away by prey that fights back. People have fought back successfully with rocks, sticks, jackets, garden tools, and their bare hands. Remain standing or try to get back up if you fall.

Chapter 31

My dream

That night I had a dream that I was running down an endless school hallway, being chased by a lion.

But not a normal lion.

A pencil lion.

Its mane wasn't made of hair, it was made of pencils.

Its claws were not normal claws, but ultra-sharpened pencil lead.

I ran and ran, but no matter how fast I pushed myself, the lion was always right on my heels.

I could smell its breath. It smelled like pencil shavings.

As I ran, I saw rows and rows of frightened students' faces watching me from the safety of their classrooms. But all the doors were locked. There was nowhere for me to hide.

Finally, as I began to tire, the lion pounced.

I turned around and looked up as the terrifying beast, every pencil on its mane trembling, opened its enormous jaws to reveal not a mouth full of teeth, but rows and rows of sharpened pencils, going as far back down its throat as I could see.

I woke up, dripping with perspiration.

That was one bad lion.

And one even badder pencil.

Chapter 32

Waking up

I awoke on the floor of my bedroom. There were pencil shavings all around me, but whether they had been there before I went to bed or whether they were from the pencil lion I couldn't be sure.

All I knew was that the pencil was bad news.

Mr. Brainfright had almost choked to death and had fallen out the window.

Fred and Clive were in the hospital.

Jack was lucky he wasn't in jail.

Gretel had broken her wrist, I'd almost lost my head, and now Jenny had been cut in half and almost eaten by a lion.

Well, Jenny being cut in half wasn't technically the pencil's fault, but everything else sure was.

What — or who — would be next?

I had to get rid of the pencil before anyone else was hurt.

The problem was that I didn't have it.

It was at school. And knowing how attached Jack was to it, I didn't think he'd take kindly to my plans to destroy it.

I'd left it in my pencil case in my desk.

I had to get to school and get rid of it before Jack arrived.

I looked at the clock.

It was 7:30 A.M.

If I hurried, I could make it.

I got up off the floor, kicked the pencil shavings under the bed, and ran out the door.

Chapter 33

Rewind

I returned to my room moments later, realizing that I still had my pajamas on.

I took my pajamas off.

I put some clothes on.

I had some breakfast.

I brushed my teeth.

And then I ran out the door and straight to school.

Chapter 34

Escaped pencil

There were only a few students in the yard when I arrived at school.

I walked up the steps, down the corridor, and into the classroom 5B.

It was still a bit messy after yesterday's lion attack. We hadn't had a chance to put the room back in order because Mr. Brainfright had given us all the rest of the day off from school (after he'd put Jenny back together again, of course).

My pencil case was sitting on top of my desk. I opened it carefully.

But the pencil wasn't inside.

Then, on a hunch, I checked Jack's desk.

I lifted the lid and, looking around to check that I was still alone, picked up Jack's pencil case.

I closed the desk lid carefully and tugged at the zipper of the pencil case.

But it didn't open.

I tugged again.

It still didn't open.

I tugged again — even harder.

This time it did open — spilling its contents all over the floor with a loud crash.

I looked up, hoping against hope that Jack wasn't standing in the doorway.

He wasn't. I still had the room to myself.

I knelt down and started scooping the pens and pencils back into Jack's pencil case.

Pens, pencils, erasers, sharpeners, markers, rulers, staplers: I couldn't believe how much stuff he managed to fit into one pencil case.

There was only one thing missing . . . my pencil!

I stood up and put the pencil case back in Jack's desk.

He must have guessed what I was going to do and had taken the pencil home for safekeeping.

I clenched my fist and punched the desk.

I was too late.

That's when I heard it — a faint sound on the far side of the room.

I looked over.

It was the pencil, rolling toward the door!

I don't know if it was still rolling from the impact of being dropped or if it was trying to escape . . . but I did know that I had to stop it before it got out that door.

I leaped across the room in one bound and landed sprawling in front of the door, just ahead of the pencil.

I looked up.

It was rolling straight toward me, and probably would have rolled right over me if I hadn't reached out and grabbed it just in time.

I shuddered.

The pencil seemed to squirm in my grasp as if it were a living thing.

Well, it wouldn't be living for much longer.

I got up and ran down the hallway and into the yard, looking for a good place to get rid of it.

But before I could do so, I saw Jack and Jenny coming through the gate on the other side of the school yard.

"Hi, Henry!" Jack called.

Oh, no!

I looked around.

There was a trash can a few feet away.

I had no choice.

I threw the pencil in and walked across the school yard to meet them.

"Hi, Jack!" I said as innocently as I could manage. "Hi, Jenny! How are you?"

"I'm all right," said Jenny. "The real question is, how are you? You seem a little upset."

"I'm fine!" I said, perhaps a little too quickly.

"Are you sure?" said Jack. "You don't look fine."

"Oh, you know," I said. "I guess I'm still a bit rattled after what happened yesterday."

Jack looked closely at me and nodded. "I guess we all are," he said. "Just think about it. Of all the schools in Northwest, the lion chose Northwest Southeast Central, and of all the classrooms in the school, it chose *ours*! Talk about bad luck!"

"Maybe it was, maybe it wasn't," I pointed out.

"What are you saying, Henry?" asked Jenny. "That it wasn't bad luck?"

"Who can say?" I told her. "And I guess it doesn't matter, anyway. It's all over now." I shrugged, suddenly feeling very light and free. The pencil was safely in the trash. It couldn't hurt anybody ever again.

Or so I thought . . .

Chapter 35

Wishes

"Well, yesterday was exciting, wasn't it?" asked Mr. Brainfright.

"Exciting?" said David. "Jenny was almost killed!"

"No thanks to you!" said Gretel.

"What do you mean by that?" said David.

"You were so scared you jumped out the window!"

David shook his head. "I didn't do it because I was scared," he said. "I went to get help!"

"By jumping out a window?" said Gretel.

"Well, I couldn't exactly go out the door, could I? There was a lion in the way!"

"All right, calm down," said Mr. Brainfright. "It's over now. And thanks to Newton's quick thinking, nobody was hurt."

Newton's face reddened. "It wasn't really quick thinking," he said. "I just got so scared when the lion roared that my arm jerked and the rabbit's foot flew out of my hand."

"Nevertheless, you managed to distract Kitty at a crucial moment, thus saving Jenny's life!" said Mr. Brainfright. "You should be very proud of yourself, Newton. Not only did you save Jenny, but you confronted nine of your top-ten fears all at the same time!"

"I'm still scared of lions, though," said Newton.

"But Jenny's alive, and that's the important thing!" said Mr. Brainfright.

"I wish it had been a pony that escaped from the circus," said Gina.

"I wish it had been a whole bunch of ponies," Penny chimed in. "Dancing ponies with plumes and sparkly saddles!"

"Speaking of ponies," said Mr. Brainfright, "how are your horses, girls?"

"The lion got them," said Gina sadly.

"Are they all right?" said Jenny.

"No," Penny reported. "They're in the hospital."

"In a *very* serious condition," Gina added.

"I'm sorry to hear that," said Mr. Brainfright.

Jack sighed and rolled his eyes. "I'm not," he said. "I'm only sorry that it wasn't a T. rex that escaped. It would have stood on the horses and then it would have squashed the whole school and we would have gotten the rest of the year off!"

"Be careful what you wish for, Jack," said Mr. Brainfright, "because it might just come true."

“That’s what my mother always says,” said Jenny.

“She’s a wise woman,” said Mr. Brainfright. “Wishes are dangerous things. Sometimes they come true, but not quite in the way you expect. My father once told me a story about a friend of his who . . . no, I can’t tell you that . . . much too frightening for a Wednesday morning.”

“Ohhhh!” groaned the class all in one voice. “Tell us! Please!”

Mr. Brainfright shook his head. “No . . . I can’t. . . . It’s really not suitable. . . .”

“Please!” we begged. “Pleeeeease!”

Mr. Brainfright looked at the door. Then he shrugged. “All right,” he said. “But don’t tell anybody I told you this . . . and don’t say I didn’t warn you!”

36

The monkey's paw

Mr. Brainfright came around to the front of his desk and leaned in close. "It happened to a friend of my father's," he began. "He was given a monkey's paw by a traveler who swore that it had the power to grant the owner three wishes."

"A monkey's *paw*?" said Fiona. "Don't monkeys have hands and feet?"

"Yes," said Mr. Brainfright, "but they are also called paws."

"Oh, I see," said Fiona, making a note.

Mr. Brainfright continued.

"Naturally my father's friend was skeptical, and who could blame him? After all, what magical properties could a monkey's paw, of all things, possess? But, nevertheless, his son urged him to try it out.

"My father's friend protested, saying he had no need of anything, but the son insisted and finally he convinced his father to wish for twenty thousand dollars to pay off the money they owed on their house. They waited and waited and waited. But nothing happened. The man put the monkey's paw on the mantelpiece, laughed about it, and went to bed.

"The following day, however, they had a visitor. It was a man from the factory where the son worked. Apparently, the son had been killed that morning in a terrible accident. His clothing had got caught in a machine and he'd been sucked into it.

"My father's friend and his wife were devastated by the news, and even more upset when the man from the company presented them with a check for twenty thousand dollars as compensation.

"You see, the man ended up getting what he wished for, but not quite in the way he'd expected to get it . . . and, indeed, in a way that he greatly wished he never had."

Mr. Brainfright drew a deep breath.

The class was completely silent.

"Is that the end of the story?" said Fiona.

"If only it had been!" said Mr. Brainfright. "But alas, no. A few weeks after the grieving parents had buried their son in a graveyard two miles from their home, the wife of the man sat up in bed and said, 'The monkey paw! We still have two wishes! Why don't we wish our son back alive again?'

"My father's friend was very reluctant — after all, the monkey paw had tricked them the first time, but his wife wouldn't be put off. He finally took the monkey paw in his hand and wished his son alive again."

"And did he come alive again?" Newton asked in a shaky voice.

"Well, no," said Mr. Brainfright.

There was a collective sigh of relief from the class.

"Not at first . . ."

There was a collective gasp.

"The man and the wife went back to bed," Mr. Brainfright continued. "But two hours later, they heard a tap at the door downstairs. 'What's that?' said the wife. 'Just rats,' said the man. 'No,' said the wife, 'it's our son! He's come back. We should have realized! The cemetery is over two miles away. It's taken him this long to walk back!'

"There was another tap . . . and another . . . and yet another . . . and before my father's friend could stop her, his wife leaped out of bed and headed downstairs.

"But not him. He had a bad feeling about this. A very bad feeling.

"Their son's body had been mangled in a machine. Given the way the monkey paw had tricked them on the first wish, even if their son *was* alive, who could tell what condition he would be in, or whether he would even really be their son?

"*Tap, tap, tap . . .*

“The man dived onto the floor, searching for where he’d dropped the monkey paw after his second wish. He had to find it before his wife opened the door!

“*Tap, tap, tap . . .*

“The man could hear his wife drawing the bolt on the front door.

“*Tap, tap, tap . . .*

“He fumbled around desperately in the darkness looking for the paw . . .

“Just as his wife was about to open the door, the man found the paw, held it tight in his hand, and wished his son, or what was left of him, dead again.

“His wife opened the door and there was nothing there except for the sound of the wind.”

As Mr. Brainfright finished his story, a collective shiver ran through the class as we imagined what might have been standing on the other side of that door.

Then, all of a sudden . . .

Chapter 37

Tap, tap, tap . . .

Tap, tap, tap . . .

There was tapping on our classroom door.

Everybody in the entire class screamed and jumped out of their chairs at the same time.

All except David Worthy.

David went even farther.

He jumped out the window . . . again!

Newton made the strange, high-pitched noise he'd made yesterday, involuntarily flinging his rabbit's foot across the room and into the face of the hall monitor, a girl from third grade, who had come to our door.

"Ouch," she said.

"Don't panic, everybody," said Mr. Brainfright, grinning. "It's just the hall monitor." He picked up Newton's rabbit's foot and tossed it back to him.

"I'll go tell David," said Jack, getting up and putting his head out the window. "It's okay, David, it's not a lion or a mangled factory worker! It's the hall monitor!"

"I knew that!" David called back. "Don't think I

was jumping out the window because I was scared. I just needed some fresh air."

"Okay, David," said Jack, smiling. "Have it your way!"

"That's enough, Jack." Mr. Brainfright chuckled as he turned to the monitor. "Now, how may we help you?"

"Sorry to interrupt," said the monitor, who looked more than a little freaked out by our class's behavior. "I was on trash duty and I found this pencil in one of the trash cans. It's a pretty good one, and, well, it has the name of one of your students on it: Henry McThrottle."

I was shocked to see the pencil again.

Very shocked.

In fact, I was so shocked that my heart actually stopped beating.

And then it started again, which was good, because if it hadn't I wouldn't have been able to write this sentence.

Or this one.

Or this one.

Or . . . well . . . you get the idea.

"Thank you," said Mr. Brainfright, taking the pencil from the monitor.

"There you are, Henry," he said, handing it to me. "I believe this is yours."

"Thank you," I said, although gratitude was the last thing I was feeling. I'd hoped never to see that pencil again.

"What was it doing in the trash?" Jack whispered. "Did you throw it away?"

"I tried to," I said. "But it obviously has other ideas!"

"Just give it to me if you don't want it!" Jack said.

"I can't," I told him. "It's too dangerous."

Jack rolled his eyes.

I rolled the pencil between my fingers.

It had my name on it. Written along the side.

The strange thing was that I didn't remember writing my name on it.

It's possible that I *did* write it, of course, but I didn't *remember* writing it. Which was weird.

But then, *everything* about this pencil was weird.

Including the fact that it was proving very difficult to get rid of.

Chapter 38

Skull Island

After eating lunch, I gave Jack the slip and headed straight for the top of Skull Island, a small hill on our school grounds. It was where we had found Mr. Greenbeard's buried treasure.

I figured that if I couldn't throw the pencil away then I'd bury it right back in the ground from where it had come.

It had lain there for at least thirty years without hurting anybody. It could lie there for another thirty as far as I was concerned.

Or, even better, thirty *thousand* years.

What I hadn't counted on, though, was how attached Jack had become to the pencil.

I'd barely scratched the surface of the ground before I realized he was behind me.

I turned and looked up at him.

"Give it to me!" he hissed, his hand out.

"No," I said, "it's too dangerous. I'm getting rid of it once and for all."

"Over my dead body," said Jack.

"If that's what it takes," I said. "Though I'm really hoping that won't be necessary."

"Give me one good reason why you have to get rid of it," Jack argued.

"One?" I said. "I can give you more than that! A lot of people have been hurt, Jack. And that's not even counting Penny's and Gina's horses, which are both in the hospital in a very serious condition!"

"Have you gone completely mad?" Jack asked. "Those horses are imaginary! And everything else you're talking about is pure coincidence! The pencil didn't make Mr. Brainfright fall out the window — he's perfectly capable of doing that himself. Fred and Clive fell off that roof because of their own stupidity — it wasn't the pencil's fault. I was standing in the wrong place at the wrong time and I got hit by a bag of money. You were standing in the wrong place at the wrong time and you got hit by a giant cardboard check! Gretel's too strong for her own good, and Jenny was attacked by a lion, not the kitten that she drew! You can't blame the pencil for any of that!"

"But the lion's name was Kitty!" I said.

"Listen to yourself, Henry. You're being ridiculous."

"No, I'm not. I'm being cautious," I said. "That's why I'm putting it back in the ground where it came from. And where it can stay. Forever!"

I turned back to continue digging.

Suddenly, I felt Jack on top of me. He pulled me backward and I fell over. I sat up to see him clutching the pencil triumphantly. Not content with the damage it had already done, the pencil had clearly taken control of Jack's mind. His eyes glowed like the ones in the skull.

"Come on, Jack," I said, getting to my feet. "Give me the pencil."

"No," said Jack. "It's mine, now! All mine!"

I took a step toward him. "Give it to me, Jack. Please."

"Keep back!" he said, threatening me with the pencil as if it were a knife.

"Don't do anything stupid, Jack," I said, taking another step toward him. "Put the pencil down, step away, and nobody will get hurt."

Jack looked at the pencil. Then he looked at me. Then he looked back at the pencil.

Then he yelled and ran straight at me, the pencil held out in front of him like a sword.

He clearly meant business.

But so did I.

I stepped out of his way, stuck my leg out, and tripped him.

He stumbled and fell headfirst onto the ground. He couldn't stop himself, and he rolled all the way to the bottom of the hill.

I ran down after him.

He was lying on his back, eyes closed, not moving but still clutching the pencil.

I pried the pencil out of his hand and stashed it safely in my jacket. I figured I'd deal with it later. For the moment I had to look after Jack.

I shook him gently. He had a graze on his forehead.

"Jack!" I said. "Are you okay?"

He blinked, spluttered, and looked straight at me.

"Who are you?" he said.

"Henry," I said. "Your friend."

"Uh-huh," he said, nodding. "And who am I?"

"Jack," I said. "Jack Japes."

"Never heard of him," he said.

Chapter 39

Mr. Grunt

I helped Jack up and, with his arm around my still-bandaged neck, guided him across the yard toward the office.

"Where are we going?" said Jack.

"I'm taking you to see Mrs. Bandaid," I told him.

"Who's Mrs. Bandaid?"

"You don't know who Mrs. Bandaid is?" I couldn't believe it. "Wow, you *are* in a bad way!"

Jack was clearly suffering from a serious case of amnesia.

Everybody knew who Mrs. Bandaid was.

She was who you went to see when you were sick or hurt.

And no matter what your problem was, she gave you Band-Aids.

Cuts, bruises, headache, sore tummy: Band-Aids . . . and lots of them, along with a big smile.

And the strange thing was that no matter whether you had a cut, a bruise, a headache, a tummyache, or any other ailment whatsoever, the Band-Aids *always* made you feel better. Or maybe it was the smile.

Whatever the case, I knew that she'd be able to fix Jack's amnesia.

On our way to Mrs. Bandaid's room, we passed the teachers' parking lot.

Mr. Grunt, our gym teacher, was standing next to his brand-new Hummer H3 — an unnecessarily huge show-offy beast of a car. In fact, *car* wasn't really the right word. It was big and solid enough to pass as an army tank.

He had an admiring group of rev-head students gathered around him.

"You've got to understand," he was saying, "that the Hummer H3 is the most powerful car ever made. It weighs over six thousand pounds, which makes it the heaviest car on the market!"

His audience burst into applause.

"Thank you," said Mr. Grunt, climbing into the front seat. "Well, can't stand around here all day. I've got some rubber to burn."

He started the car.

It gave a deep, throaty roar and blasted a thick dark cloud of smoke out behind it. Then, burning rubber, with all four tires squealing and smoking, Mr. Grunt fishtailed wildly out of the parking lot and tore off down the road, tooting his horn all the way to make sure as many students as possible noticed him.

The crowd of students applauded one last time and

then went back to their sad little lives, waiting for Mr. Grunt to return.

I shook my head at what a show-off Mr. Grunt was. His gym classes mainly consisted of him giving demonstrations about how to perform a particular activity. Sometimes the demonstration went on for the whole period and the only exercise we would get was changing into our gym clothes at the beginning of the lesson and changing back out of them at the end. This was better than when we actually *did* get to do the activity, though, because Mr. Grunt usually took it as an opportunity to criticize our efforts and to point out all the ways in which we couldn't do it as well as he could.

"Who was that?" asked Jack.

"Mr. Grunt," I told him.

"He's a show-off."

"You got that right."

As I watched Mr. Grunt's Hummer disappear into the distance, an idea began to form.

It was obviously going to take more than a trash can or a hole in the ground to get rid of the pencil.

I figured that six thousand pounds worth of Hummer might just do the trick.

All I had to do was wait until the end of the day and sneak the pencil underneath one of the Hummer's tires. Before long, that pencil would be nothing more than a bad memory.

But first I had to get Jack to Mrs. Bandaid.

Chapter 40

Mrs. Rosethorn

Unfortunately, you couldn't just go straight to Mrs. Bandaid's room.

You had to get past Mrs. Rosethorn first.

I got Jack up the steps and into the school office.

"What do you want?" Mrs. Rosethorn spat out, glaring at us.

"Who are you?" Jack asked.

Mrs. Rosethorn glared at him even harder. If his brain hadn't already been wiped clean by the fall, her laserlike stare would have done it for him.

Jack gazed at her blankly.

"We need to see Mrs. Bandaid," I said.

"We need to see Mrs. Bandaid *what*?" Mrs. Rosethorn snapped.

"We need to see Mrs. Bandaid, *please*. Could you let her know that we're here?"

"What do you need to see her for?"

"See who?" said Jack.

"Mrs. Bandaid," Mrs. Rosethorn answered impatiently. "What do you need to see her for?"

"Jack's had an accident," I told her. "I think it's serious."

Mrs. Rosethorn looked at Jack's forehead. "It's only a scratch," she sniffed. "Don't waste Mrs. Bandaid's time with that."

"It's more than a scratch," I said.

"Are you arguing with me, young man?"

"No," I said, "but it's definitely more than a scratch. He can't remember *anything*."

"Of course he can," Mrs. Rosethorn said dismissively. "He's just wasting everybody's time. Go outside and play. The fresh air will do you both good."

I waited.

Mrs. Rosethorn glared.

"Well, what are you waiting for?" she finally asked.

"For you to let Mrs. Bandaid know we're here," I said. "Or should I go and get my friend Gretel?"

Gretel and Mrs. Rosethorn had a history. I thought this might work.

It did.

"No, it's all right," Mrs. Rosethorn said, her voice shaking a little. "I'll tell her." She picked up the phone. "Just wait there. And don't get into any trouble. . . . I've got my eye on you!"

Somehow, against all odds, Jack and I managed to keep out of trouble for the two minutes it took for Mrs. Bandaid to arrive.

"Oh, you poor thing," she said the moment she saw Jack. She ushered him gently into her room.

Then she went to town on him.

By the time she was finished, Jack's head was practically covered in Band-Aids. The only parts of his face not covered were his eyes and mouth.

Jack said he definitely felt better, but he still wasn't sure who Mrs. Bandaid was, who I was, or even who he was, so Mrs. Bandaid called his parents to come and pick him up.

The pencil's victims were mounting at a fast rate.

Mr. Brainfright, me, Clive, Fred, Jenny, Penny's horse, Gina's horse, and now Jack.

Who would be next?

Well, *nobody* if I could help it.

And I had a pretty good idea of how to do that.

Chapter 41

Hummer time

When the bell for the end of school rang, I bolted down to the parking lot. I had to get there before Mr. Grunt's fan club arrived to wish him farewell for the day.

I took the pencil out of my pocket and wedged it underneath the left rear tire. The tire looked more like a tractor's than a car's — a fact that I was very happy about. I knew the pencil wasn't going to give in without a fight, but judging by the size and width of the tire, this was one fight it wasn't going to win.

I tried not to look at the skull eraser as I walked away, but I couldn't help it.

It looked angry, its little black eyes boring straight into me.

I walked across the parking lot to a row of bushes. I could hide in them and see the pencil crushed with my own eyes.

I didn't want to leave anything to chance.

It didn't take long for Mr. Grunt's fan club to appear. There were about half a dozen of them. Their chief topic of conversation was what spectacular move Mr. Grunt would use to leave the parking lot this afternoon. Would he burn rubber, do a 360-degree spin, or would he lift the front wheels off the ground and drive out on the back ones?

I wanted to yell, "Get a life!" but I didn't. Not only would it have given away the fact that I was hiding in the bushes, it would have suggested that I, too, needed to get a life, since I got my kicks by hiding in the bushes, spying on other losers with no lives. Which was *obviously* not the case.

I could hear Mr. Grunt approaching, whistling and jangling the keys he kept on a long gold chain.

"Good afternoon, boys," he said to the group.

"Good afternoon, Mr. Grunt," they said.

Mr. Grunt clicked his key lock and the doors opened with a bleep.

He got into his car, started up the engine, and pumped the accelerator a few times. The Hummer roared.

Mr. Grunt leaned out the driver's-side window.

"Stand back, boys," he said, "and I'll show you something special!"

The boys all did as he suggested.

Mr. Grunt pumped the accelerator again, filling the parking lot with exhaust fumes. Then he reversed out of his parking space at high speed.

I shut my eyes and listened as hard as I could for the crushing of the pencil above the noise of the car's engine.

But I couldn't hear any crushing.

All I could hear was a weird scraping noise that was getting louder . . . and louder . . . and louder!

I opened my eyes.

To my horror, Mr. Grunt's Hummer was skidding out of control . . . straight toward the bush I was hiding in!

Chapter 42

Grunt versus Cross

I leaped from the bush just in time.

The Hummer flattened not just the bush I was hiding in, but the entire row of bushes! It took out a fire hydrant and a flower bed, and didn't stop until it smashed into the side of a small green hatchback.

Now, of all the small green hatchbacks that you could smash into, this was the very one that you definitely would *not* want to smash into. Because this small green hatchback belonged to Mrs. Cross. And Mrs. Cross could get very cross indeed.

The door of the hatchback opened and Mrs. Cross got out.

Not surprisingly, she looked cross. Very cross.

"Grunt!" she said. "Look what you've done!"

Mr. Grunt's fan club took fright at the sight of Mrs. Cross being so cross and ran away.

Mr. Grunt probably would have *liked* to run away, but he couldn't. He seemed quite dazed and very unsteady on his feet as he climbed down from his Hummer. "I'm so sorry, Mrs. Cross," he said. "I don't know what happened!"

"You were driving too fast!" said Mrs. Cross. "That's what happened! You are *always* driving too fast! It makes me very cross! We're not driving bumper cars, you know!"

"No, Mrs. Cross," said Mr. Grunt. "I know that . . . and I'm very sorry. It's just that I completely lost control . . ."

"Yes, because you were *driving too fast*!" repeated Mrs. Cross.

"Maybe, but that's not why I lost control. One of my back wheels — I think it was the left — seemed to lose contact with the ground."

"Well," said Mrs. Cross, "when you're driving as fast as you do, that's bound to happen, you silly man."

Mr. Grunt bent down to examine his tire. "It felt like something was stuck in it . . . a stick or something like a stick, perhaps . . ."

Suddenly, I understood what must have happened.

The pencil had not been crushed.

It had sabotaged Mr. Grunt's tire!

And he was about to find it, and when he did find it he'd see my name on it, and then . . . well, to tell you the truth, I didn't want to think about "and then."

I had to get that pencil before he did.

Luckily, Mrs. Cross wasn't through with Mr. Grunt yet. "Now listen to me, Grunt," she said. "And have the good manners to look at a person when she is speaking to you. There's nothing wrong with your back tire. I know that and you know that. We both know why you crashed, don't we? Because you are an irresponsible, selfish, self-centered driver with no regard for the rights of others on the road or anywhere else as far as I can see!"

Mrs. Cross was really letting him have it.

While she did so, I managed to crawl under the car, grab my pencil, and then get out of there without either of them seeing me. As I ran I could still hear Mrs. Cross.

"And another thing, Grunt . . ." she was saying.

I almost felt sorry for Mr. Grunt. I had plenty of problems of my own, including a killer pencil that had it in for me and my friends, but I sure wouldn't have traded places with Mr. Grunt at that moment for anything!

Chapter 43

Welcome back, Mr. Spade

That night I had another bad dream. This time it was about Hummers with pencil teeth and spiky pencil wheels chasing me around the school yard.

I awoke on the floor again, dripping with sweat and shaking.

I had to get rid of that pencil . . . but how?

The next day at school, Principal Greenbeard called a special whole-school assembly.

We all gathered in the school auditorium, the teachers arranged at strategic points around the room.

Everyone was there.

The grade teachers: Mr. Naughtychair, Miss Sweet, Mr. Highfive, Mrs. Spectacles, Mr. Brainfright, and Mrs. Cross.

All the other teachers: Mrs. Rainbow the art teacher, Mr. Shush the librarian, and Mr. Grunt the show-off . . . I mean, gym teacher.

Mr. Grunt appeared to have recovered from Mrs. Cross's scolding yesterday afternoon, although she still shot him the occasional cross glance across the stage.

And speaking of cross glances, Mrs. Rosethorn was there as well, glowering at the audience. I don't think she approved of assemblies. She probably thought they were a waste of time. And I'd have to agree that in this instance she was right.

Mrs. Bandaid was there, clutching a handful of Band-Aids. Although the risk of physical injury during school assemblies was fairly low, I guess there was always the danger of a student — or teacher — passing out during one of Principal Greenbeard's longer speeches and hitting his or her head on the floor.

Even Mr. Spade, the school gardener, was there, looking much more relaxed than the last time I'd seen him. He'd been very upset about all the hole-digging that went on when practically every student in the school was looking for Greenbeard's treasure. He'd gotten so upset, in fact, that he'd had to go on a stress leave.

Which — as it eventually turned out — was the main reason for the assembly.

Principal Greenbeard, resplendent in a brilliant white naval uniform, was droning on and on about how the school was like a big ship and how he saw himself as the captain of that ship and how it was his responsibility to guide us all safely through the unpredictable and sometimes very dangerous sea of life, and how it was our responsibility to all pull together, to hoist the sails and man the paddles and plug the leaks and all hands on deck and yo-ho-ho three bottles of rum on a dead man's chest . . . well, I may have drifted off a little bit there, but as far as I could make out, that was the general gist of it. But before it got to the point where I passed out, slumped over, and hit my head on the floor, he got to the main item on the agenda, which was to welcome Mr. Spade back aboard after his "shore leave."

"And just to show you how much we appreciate your work aboard the good ship *Northwest Southeast Central*, we're delighted that the school's recent 'build your own boat' fund-raising effort has allowed us to buy the new Mighty Boy trash compactor you always wanted!"

Principal Greenbeard motioned for Mr. Spade to come up onstage.

There was a round of applause as Mr. Spade walked up to the podium. He was clearly overwhelmed with Principal Greenbeard's thoughtfulness and was wiping away tears as he and Principal Greenbeard warmly saluted each other.

"On behalf of the whole crew of the good ship *Northwest Southeast Central*," said Principal Greenbeard, "I hereby welcome you back and officially present you with the instruction manual for the

Mighty Boy trash compactor!" He put a manual the size of a telephone book into Mr. Spade's hand.

Jack, who was sitting beside me, tapped my arm. He was back at school, even though he was still suffering from temporary amnesia. The doctors thought that the best chance for him to recover his memory was to be in familiar surroundings with familiar people.

"Who's that?" he whispered.

"Mr. Spade," I said. "He's the groundskeeper."

Mr. Spade shuffled over to the microphone. "I'd like to thank you all for your very kind gesture," he said. "It's great to be back, and the Mighty Boy's five hundred thousand pounds of brute trash-compacting force will help me get the school grounds into tip-top shape as fast as possible!"

There was another round of applause.

I was fully awake now.

Five hundred thousand pounds of brute trash-compacting force.

I could use that!

As if reading my mind, Principal Greenbeard chose that moment to remind us all that Mr. Spade's shed — and the Mighty Boy trash compactor — were strictly out of bounds. "Any scurvy dogs breaking this rule will be thrown into the brig and will go without food and water for a week. Do I make myself clear?"

We all nodded.

"I'd also like to take this opportunity to welcome Fred and Clive Durkin back to school after their recent stay in the hospital. We wish you both a speedy recovery."

I turned around.

Sure enough, Fred and Clive were sitting a few rows behind me. Clive had his leg in a cast, and Fred had his arm in a sling.

There was a round of applause to welcome them back.

But I didn't join in.

Jenny elbowed me. "Henry!" she said. "You're not being very nice!"

"They've never been very nice to me," I pointed out.

Jenny sighed.

"Who are Clive and Fred?" asked Jack.

"They're not very nice," I explained.

"Henry!" said Jenny.

I shrugged.

"Now we shall all sing the school song," announced Principal Greenbeard.

Now this was something we *did* like.

We all joined in a rousing version of "The Good Ship *Lollipop*," Except that when we got to the word "*Lollipop*" we sang "*Northwest Southeast Central*" instead.

It was pretty crazy, but we all enjoyed it. In fact, it was definitely the best thing about school assemblies.

I patted the pencil in my pocket.

"We're going on a little trip, you and me," I said.

Chapter 44

Mighty Boy

As we left the hall, I overheard Principal Greenbeard inviting Mr. Spade back to his office for a cup of tea.

This was my chance.

I had to act fast.

I nudged Jenny.

"What is it?" she asked.

"I'll be a little late back to class," I said.

"Why?"

"I've got an errand to do."

"What sort of errand?"

"Can't say."

Jenny noticed me looking at Mr. Spade's shed.

She shook her head. "I know exactly what you're going to do," she said. "And it's completely against the school rules! You heard Principal Greenbeard. If you get caught in there, your life won't be worth living!"

I told her about how I'd almost been run over by Mr. Grunt's Hummer. When I finished, Jenny nodded.

"All right," she said, perhaps remembering her

own experience with the pencil's evil sense of humor. "But I'm coming with you."

"Jenny!" I said. "No! I need you to cover for me in class. Besides, it's too dangerous."

"Yeah," said Jenny, "too dangerous for you to do it alone. I'm coming with you and that's that. We'll just chuck the pencil in, turn on the compactor, and be back in class before anyone has even noticed that we're missing."

"Okay," I said. I knew there was no point in arguing. Jenny can be really stubborn when she wants to be. And she was right — it wasn't going to take long.

We dropped to the back of the line, and as the rest of the class turned the corner to head toward our classroom, Jenny and I turned in the opposite direction and headed for Mr. Spade's shed.

We approached it warily, making sure that nobody saw us.

After one last look around, we slipped inside.

Standing in the middle of the shed was Mr. Spade's new Mighty Boy trash compactor.

A solid block of gleaming steel.

The specifications on the side boasted six-inch hydraulic pistons and five hundred thousand pounds of brute trash-compacting force.

If that couldn't deal with my pencil, then nothing could.

"Well, what are you waiting for, Henry?" Jenny asked. "Put it in!"

"I will!" I said, studying the control panel. "I'm just trying to figure out how to turn it on. Mr. Spade's got the instruction manual, remember? Where's Grant Gadget when you need him?"

"What about this button here?" Jenny pointed to a large green button with the word ON written on it.

"Of course," I said, "I was getting to that. I was just trying to figure out how to get the pencil inside the compactor first."

"What about this chute?" said Jenny. "It's labeled PLACE SMALL ITEMS HERE."

Gee, I had to hand it to her. Jenny really knew her way around a Mighty Boy trash compactor.

"Good work," I said, taking the pencil out of my pocket and passing it to her. "You put it in and I'll turn it on."

Jenny took the pencil and nodded. "Now?" she said.

"Now!"

She dropped the pencil down the chute.

I pushed the button.

The compactor began to vibrate — quietly at first, and then increasing in volume until it was really humming.

And then it started to compact.

We could hear it smashing, grinding, and pulverizing.

I could hardly believe it. "It's working!" I yelled above the noise. "It's really working! It's destroying the pencil! At last!"

"That's great," Jenny said. "I just can't help feeling a tiny bit sorry for it, though."

"Are you kidding?!" I yelled. "That pencil was bad news! It wanted us all dead . . . and it almost succeeded . . . and you feel sorry for it?"

Jenny shrugged. "I know I shouldn't," she said. "I just can't help it."

We watched as the Mighty Boy compacted away. *That pencil must be nothing but splinters by now*, I thought.

"Do you think it's done yet?" Jenny asked.

"Yeah," I told her. "It must be. I'll turn it off. I just can't see where the switch is."

"How about this red button that says OFF?"

"Do you have one of these at home?" I asked.

"No!" She laughed. "It's just really easy to operate!"

"Then why did it come with that enormous manual?" I said, pushing the OFF button.

"Beats me."

Even though I turned it off, the Mighty Boy

kept right on compacting. In fact, it seemed to be increasing its intensity. It was starting to shudder violently, so much so that it was actually moving across the floor.

I punched the OFF button again. And again. And again.

But it still didn't turn off.

"Turn it off, Henry!" Jenny screamed.

"I'm trying to," I hollered back. "But it's not responding."

"Here," said Jenny, pushing me out of the way. "Let me try!" She pounded on the button, but the only response was it kept getting louder and louder.

As it moved across the floor toward us, we were being pushed back into a corner of the shed, only we didn't notice this, because we were so intent on pushing the OFF button.

Well, we didn't notice until it was too late.

"Henry!" cried Jenny, hitting me on the arm. "We can't get out! We're trapped!"

I looked up. She was right.

The Mighty Boy had pushed us into a corner. It was coming closer and closer.

We were going to be crushed against the wall!

"Push!" I yelled.

With our arms outstretched, we pushed against it as hard as we could.

But it was no use.

The Mighty Boy was too heavy. Too powerful. We couldn't hold it off.

We were just sliding across the floor.

Sliding to our *doom*.

Chapter 45

Mighty girl

That's when we heard Gretel.

"Henry!" she called. "Jenny! Where are you?"

"Over here!" we called. "Behind the compactor!"

I don't know how we heard her, or how she heard us above the noise, but hear us she did. The next thing we knew, she leaped over the top of the machine and was standing between us.

"I can't leave you two alone for a minute!" she said, pushing against the machine with her one good hand.

"We were just trying to get rid of the pencil!" said Jenny.

"Really?" said Gretel, laughing. "Looks like the other way around to me!"

"Stop laughing," I said. "This is serious!"

"I know," said Gretel, "but so am I!"

At that, she stopped laughing and began to grimace as she pushed the machine back toward the center of the room, despite the fact that one of her arms was in a sling.

Jenny and I looked at each other.

We'd known Gretel was strong — she was the strongest person in the school — but we hadn't known that she was *this* strong.

As she pushed, though, the machine seemed to go into overdrive.

The grinding noise changed to a rattling and clanking sound.

Smoke started pouring out of its bottom.

Bits started falling off. First buttons, then handles, then, to our astonishment, whole panels!

Nuts, bolts, and springs were flying through the air.

"Take cover!" Gretel yelled. "I think it's going to blow up!"

We ran for the safety of a workbench and took shelter behind it.

The Mighty Boy gave one mighty shudder and then disintegrated in front of our eyes.

We were left looking at nothing but a pile of smoking metal.

And wouldn't you know it, lying in the middle of all that metallic rubble was the pencil.

Completely intact.

Chapter 46

Killer pencil

After retrieving the pencil, we left the remains of the not-so-mighty Mighty Boy on the floor of the shed and headed back to class.

"Poor Mr. Spade," said Jenny. "He's going to be very upset."

"Yes," said Gretel. "I suspect he's going to be needing some more shore leave when he sees that mess."

"Poor Mr. Spade?" I said. "His stupid trash compactor almost compacted us!"

"It wasn't Mr. Spade's fault *or* the compactor's," Gretel pointed out. "It was the pencil's!"

"You're right," I said. "This pencil is evil. It would have killed us if you hadn't come along."

"You saved our lives!" Jenny exclaimed.

Gretel shrugged. "I did what I had to do."

"But how did you know where we were?" Jenny asked.

"I noticed you weren't in class when Mr. Brainfright called the roll," Gretel replied. "I answered for you, and then I asked if I could go to the bathroom. It wasn't hard to figure out where you were. I just followed the noise!"

We managed to slip back into class without Mr. Brainfright seeing us. He was involved in a deep discussion with Penny and Gina about the best food for horses.

"It's *ice cream*, I tell you," he was saying. "Horses *love* ice cream!"

"No, they don't," said Gina. "Horses eat *hay*."

"And chaff," said Penny. "Horses love chaff."

"Not as much as they love ice cream," said Mr. Brainfright.

"I've never seen a horse eating ice cream," Gina sniffed.

"Me neither," Penny added.

"That's because they have trouble holding the spoon!" said Mr. Brainfright. "Their hooves aren't made for it. . . ." and so on and so on. Mr. Brainfright could argue with anyone about *anything*.

Chapter 47

Mr. Brainfright's important lesson no. 4

Horses love ice cream but the reason you don't see horses eating ice cream is because they have trouble holding the spoon. Their hooves aren't made for it.

Chapter 48

A bold idea

As we sat down, Clive eyed us suspiciously.

"Where have you all been?" he asked.

"Nowhere," I said.

"Yes, you have," he said. "You've been *somewhere*."

"Darn," I said to Jenny and Gretel. "He's too smart for us!"

We went over to the reading corner, where Newton was sitting.

He looked at us nervously. "Is everything all right?"

"No," I replied. "Not really."

I told him about our run-in with the Mighty Boy and my near miss with Mr. Grunt's Hummer.

Newton nodded thoughtfully. "So every time you try to get rid of the pencil something bad happens to you?"

"That's right," I said.

"And you're trying to get rid of it because every time you draw somebody with the pencil — even if it's a picture of something nice — something bad happens to the person?"

"Right again."

Newton nodded. "So maybe the only thing that can destroy the pencil is the pencil itself."

"That's a very good idea, Newton," said Jenny. "Don't you think so, Henry?"

"Just one problem," I said. "I don't think the pencil is about to destroy itself."

"No," said Newton, "but what if you used the pencil to draw something bad happening to the pencil?"

"Then I'm the one who would suffer!" I said.

"Maybe not, Henry," said Gretel. "Not if you didn't draw *yourself*. Just the pencil!"

I thought about what Newton and Gretel were saying.

I could see what they were getting at . . . but it was dangerous.

I heard neighing. I turned around. Jack was on his hands and knees. Penny and Gina were riding on his back, using a jump rope as reins.

"Giddyup, Ponyboy," said Gina. "Giddyup."

It was a sad sight.

The pencil had reduced Jack to a beast of burden. And to think, he'd been the only one trying to save it!

Newton and Gretel's idea was dangerous, sure, but it was all we had.

"Let's do it," I said, taking the pencil out of my pocket.

Chapter 49

Drawing the pencil's doom

This is what I drew.

Frame #1: The pencil lying at the bottom of a cliff.

Frame #2: A 50 million billion–ton boulder at the top of the cliff.

Frame #3: A butterfly flies past the boulder.

Frame #4: The air from the butterfly's wings dislodges the boulder.

Frame #5: The boulder rolls off the edge of the cliff.

Frame #6: The boulder falls.

Frame #7: And falls.

Frame #8: And falls.

Frame #9: The pencil looks up.

Frame #10: The boulder smashes down on top of the pencil.

Frame #11: The boulder rolls away and all that is left of the pencil is a little pile of dust.

Frame #12: The butterfly flies past. The wind from its wings makes the pencil dust fly up into the air and disappear.

Chapter 50

The pencil's doom

"That is *so* good, Henry!" said Jenny.

"It is!" said Gretel. "Really good!"

"I'm scared," said Newton, backing away from the table.

"But it was your idea!" I said.

"I know," Newton admitted. "But I'm still scared! What if the pencil finds out?"

"It won't," I promised him. "And even if it does, it's doomed!"

"It's an excellent drawing, Henry," said a voice behind us. "Better than the one that Jack drew, that's for sure."

We all turned around.

Clive Durkin was behind us, leaning on his crutches.

"What do you want, Clive?" I said.

"Just admiring your drawing," he said. "There's no law against that, is there?"

"No," said Gretel, "but there *is* a law against snooping."

"I'm not snooping!" said Clive.

"How long have you been there?" I asked.

"Long enough," said Clive, a slight smile playing around his lips.

"What's that supposed to mean?" Gretel snarled.

"Nothing," said Clive, hoisting himself back onto his crutches.

He began crutching his way toward his desk. "See ya!"

"Well?" said Jenny, as we watched him go. "What happens now?"

"We wait," I told her.

"For how long?"

"As long as it takes," I said.

Which, as it turned out, wasn't very long at all, thanks to Clive.

Chapter 51

Mr. Grunt demonstrates

Halfway through the morning we had gym class with Mr. Grunt.

I put the pencil in my locker, took out my gym bag, and got changed.

It was one of Mr. Grunt's "demonstration" classes.

Our annual interschool track-and-field meet was coming up, and Mr. Grunt wanted us to be thoroughly familiar with all the events.

For one hour we watched Mr. Grunt demonstrate how to start a running race from the crouch position, how to throw a shot put, how to throw a javelin, how to throw a discus, how to high-jump, how to triple-jump, how to long-jump, and how to stand on a winner's dais without falling off.

Then he told us all to go and get changed back into our school uniforms and that he'd demonstrate some more stuff for us in the next class.

It was definitely something to look forward to.

"I'm scared," said Newton, as we walked back down the corridor toward our lockers.

"What are you scared about?" I asked.

"What if the pencil finds out that turning its power against itself was my idea?"

"Don't worry about it," I said. "It doesn't matter what that pencil thinks anymore. It's doomed!"

Newton didn't look convinced. "I'm still scared," he said.

"You can be if you want," I said, putting my arm around his shoulder. "But there's absolutely nothing to be scared about!"

That's when I noticed my locker door.

It was completely smashed in, covered in dents . . . the sort of dents that might have been made with, oh, let's see . . . the end of a crutch!

I didn't have to look inside the locker to know what that meant.

Our plan to turn the pencil's power against itself had been a good plan, but what we'd forgotten was, that like the monkey paw's wishes, the pencil's drawings had a habit of coming true in unexpected ways.

We'd been tricked again. The pencil had disappeared all right . . . but not quite in the way we'd intended. It had been stolen!

And there were no prizes for guessing who was responsible.

Although I'd just assured Newton that there was absolutely nothing to be scared about, I knew that the exact opposite was now true.

With the pencil of doom in Clive's hands, there was *everything* to be scared about.

"I'm scared," Newton said again, looking at the wreckage of my locker.

"Me too," I told him.

Chapter 52

Break in!

I stared at my locker.

I took a few deep breaths as I tried to figure out what to do.

Clive was not exactly the sharpest pencil in the pencil case. He had no idea of the true power of the pencil he'd stolen. With a few careless strokes, he could wreak havoc and destruction on an enormous scale. The fate of the school, and possibly the entire world, was at stake.

Just then, Jenny, Jack, and Gretel came along the corridor.

Jenny gasped when she saw my locker. "How could anyone *do* such a thing?" she said.

"Easy," I told her. "He just gets his crutch and pounds it against the door over and over until the door caves in."

"No, I don't mean that. I mean, how could anyone be so mean to a locker door?"

"You'd better ask Clive Durkin," I said.

"You think Clive did it?" said Jack. "He seems like a nice guy to me."

"He's *not* nice," I said. "I told you at the assembly, remember?"

Jack looked at me blankly. "No," he said.

Poor Jack. His memory loss was worse than I thought.

"I *know* he did it," I assured everyone.

Gretel frowned. "He couldn't have," she said.

"Why not?" I asked.

"He was with us!"

"No, he wasn't," I told her. "He got out of gym because of his broken leg. Mr. Brainfright told him to go to the library instead."

"Henry's right," said Jenny. "I saw him as we walked past."

"When?" I asked.

"Just now!"

"What was he doing?"

"I didn't really pay that much attention." Jenny thought about it for a moment. "He looked like he was working on something."

Her words chilled me to the core.

We were really in trouble.

Clive never *worked* in the library. He spent all his time annoying everybody else. If he was actually working, it could mean only one thing — he was using the pencil to draw a cartoon. And I had no doubt that it would feature all of us.

"There's no time to waste!" I said. "We've got to stop him!"

"Count me in," said Gretel. "I've still got one good arm."

"I'll come with you," Jack volunteered. "I promised those nice horsey girls I'd meet them in the library."

"I'm coming, too," said Newton. "I'm too scared to stay here all on my own!"

"You're not going to do anything nasty to Clive, are you?" Jenny asked.

"Not if we can avoid it," I told her. "But we're going to have to do whatever it takes. And I'm pretty sure he's getting ready to do something nasty to us."

"I don't care," said Jenny. "Two wrongs don't make a right! I'm going to come along and make sure you all play nice!"

"We're not playing!" I said. "Don't you get it? This is for real!"

The lunch bell rang.

"Showtime!" I said.

Chapter 53

Spying on Clive

We all regrouped outside the library.

All of us, that is, except Jack, who went in to find Gina and Penny. Not only had he lost his memory, but apparently his mind as well.

Through the window, we could see Clive at one of the group study tables, bent over and using the pencil.

"All right," I said. "We have to be smart about this. We can't just all walk in there at the same time."

"Why not?" said Gretel.

"Because he might panic and do something stupid," I said. "I mean, *draw* something stupid."

"Good point," said Gretel.

I studied the layout of the library carefully. The study tables were grouped at one end. Behind these there were eight shelves of books in a line and then some spinning racks and computers.

"We have to infiltrate the library quietly," I said. "One at a time. We'll meet behind the first shelf in the row, the one next to Clive's table so we can see exactly what he's drawing. I'll go first. Give me thirty seconds to get into position and then the next person come in after that. Right?"

Everybody nodded.

I entered the library.

Mr. Shush was sitting at the desk. He looked up when I came in and put his finger to his lips. "Shush," he said.

I nodded and sneaked across to the shelf behind where Clive was sitting.

Gretel was next, followed by Newton, and then Jenny.

Clive was so involved in his drawing that he didn't look up.

He didn't even look up when Penny and Gina got told off by Mr. Shush for riding Jack around the study tables.

"This is a library, not a racetrack," he reminded the girls for about the one million five hundred and sixty-first time.

Penny and Gina nodded solemnly and went to ride Jack at the end of the row of shelves where Mr. Shush couldn't see them.

Meanwhile, we were all assembled behind the shelf nearest to Clive's table.

"Shush," I said to the group. "Nobody make a sound!"

I pushed a couple of books aside to get a peek at Clive's cartoon.

It was worse than I could possibly have imagined.

Clive had drawn a four-frame cartoon called, “AVALANCHE! Starring Henry McThrottle, Jack Japes, Gretel Armstrong, Newton Hooton, and Jenny Friendly.”

Chapter 54

"AVALANCHE! Starring Henry McThrottle, Jack Japes, Gretel Armstrong, Newton Hooton, and Jenny Friendly"

Frame #1: Me, Jack, Gretel, Newton, and Jenny are all sitting on a blanket having a picnic at the bottom of a snowcapped mountain.

Frame #2: The cap of the snowcapped mountain breaks off.

Frame #3: We are all buried underneath the cap of the snowcapped mountain.

Frame #4: Five tombstones in a ring on the snow — a tombstone for each one of us!

Chapter 55

Things get worse than they already were

I motioned for everybody to crouch down.

"We're doomed!" said Newton.

"Only if we think like that," I said. "We've got to do something!"

"I say we charge Clive, grab the cartoon, and rip it to pieces!" whispered Gretel.

"It's too late for that," I said. "He's already drawn it."

"Perhaps if we were to ask him nicely to erase it?" said Jenny.

"This is Clive Durkin we're dealing with," I hissed. "He doesn't even know the meaning of the word *nice*."

Then, just when I thought things couldn't possibly get any worse than they already were, they did!

Fred Durkin came into the library and walked up to Clive's table.

"Hi, Clive," he said. "How come you're in here? It's lunchtime!"

"Yeah, I know," said Clive. "But I stole this pencil off McThrottle."

Fred chuckled. "You stole a *pencil*? Why?"

"It's no ordinary pencil," said Clive. "It's got magic powers. Whatever you draw with it comes true!"

"Oh, a *magic* pencil," said Fred. "Well, that explains it. Can I just ask one question?"

"What?" said Clive.

"You sure you didn't land on your head when you fell off the roof?"

"No!" said Clive. "I know it sounds crazy, but it's true. And our accident was no accident, either."

"I know that," said Fred. "It was all *your* fault."

"No," said Clive, "it wasn't my fault at all. It was the pencil's. I overheard them talking. Apparently, Jack Japes used this pencil to draw that cartoon of us parachuting and landing on top of each other, and that's why we had the accident."

Fred laughed. "I think they're putting you on, little brother. That's just a coincidence."

"No, it's true, Fred!" said Clive. "So, to get revenge I stole it and drew this cartoon of them getting buried in an avalanche."

Fred took the cartoon from Clive and examined it.

"That's a pretty good drawing," he said. "I didn't know you could draw that well."

"I can't!" said Clive. "That's what I'm trying to tell you! It's the pencil. It's like it does the drawing itself!"

"Oooooh, spooky!" Fred waved the pencil in front of Clive's face.

"Yeah, it is spooky," said Clive, missing Fred's sarcasm. "They're all terrified of it!"

"Oh, so *that's* why they're all hiding behind the shelf," said Fred.

We froze.

Darn! He knew we were here!

None of us said anything, as if by being really quiet he would just forget all about us.

"I know you're there," said Fred, coming and standing at the end of the shelf.

"I'm scared!" whispered Newton.

"We all are!" I whispered back.

"Is this what you're scared of?" said Fred, waving the pencil at us. "This spooky-wooky little pencil? With its scary little skull eraser? Ooooohhhhhh!"

Chapter 56

Avalanche!

"It's no joke, Fred," I said. "You don't know what you're messing with!"

"Is that a fact?" Fred taunted. "Well, you didn't know who *you* were messing with when Jack drew that cartoon of me and Clive."

"I swear we didn't know the power of the pencil when Jack drew that!" I said.

"Too bad," said Fred. "You shouldn't have been drawing disrespectful cartoons of me in the first place. I've got feelings, too, you know."

"Really?" Gretel asked.

"Nah, just kidding," said Fred, laughing at his little joke.

But not as much as Clive, who was practically killing himself laughing. "You crack me up, Fred!" he guffawed.

"I'll crack you up if you don't stop laughing," said Fred, the smile completely faded from his face. "It's not *that* funny!"

"SHUSH!" said Mr. Shush.

"Sorry, Mr. Shush!" said Fred. "I'm just having a word with them now."

"Thank you, Frederick," said Mr. Shush.

Mr. Shush, like all the other teachers in the school, was under the mistaken impression that Fred Durkin was a model student.

Suddenly, there was a huge crash.

Followed by another huge crash.

And another.

And another!

Fred gasped, dropped the pencil, and jumped backward.

There was another huge crash, and then the shelf on our right began to tip toward us, dropping all its books on top of us and all around us before crashing into the shelf on our left and pushing it over as well.

Everything went dark.

Chapter 57

Buried alive

I blinked.

It was dark.

I blinked again.

It was still dark.

Dark was bad. But blinking was good. It meant I was still alive.

But was anybody else?

It appeared that we were trapped underneath the combined weight of seven bookshelves and all the books that had been on them.

I desperately wanted to call out, but the weight of books crushing down on me was making it almost impossible to breathe, let alone speak. Of course, there was also the fact that we were in the library and that calling out was strictly against Mr. Shush's rules. Even so, though, it was the not-being-able-to-breathe that was the main thing stopping me from calling out.

I tried to move my legs, but they were pinned tight.

My arms were, too, except for the fingers on my right hand.

I wiggled my fingers, desperately trying to free up enough space to move my hand.

Eventually, I managed to do that, and then I worked on freeing up enough space to move my arm.

I was panting and gasping with the effort, but I had no choice. I had to keep going. I wasn't going to let the pencil win.

After what seemed like minutes of painstaking effort I got my arm free, and was able to make relatively fast progress removing the books around me to form a small but substantial space to move in.

"Hello?" said a voice.

It was Newton.

"Newton!" I said. "Where are you?"

"I don't know," he said. "Where are you?"

"Here," I said.

"Where's here?" said Newton.

I could hear Newton's voice coming from just in front of me. I pulled some books out of the way and there he was.

By now my eyes had adjusted to the darkness and I could make out his sad, scared little face.

"Are you all right?" I asked.

"I think so," Newton replied. "What happened?"

"It was an avalanche!" I said. "Of books."

Clive's cartoon of us being buried in an avalanche had come true.

It just hadn't come about in quite the way they'd intended.

We'd been buried in an avalanche all right, but not an avalanche of snow . . . an avalanche of books!

"I'm scared," said Newton.

"At least you're alive," I told him.

"Yes," he said, "but is anybody else?"

"I am!" said Gretel, removing a stack of books and pushing her head into our space.

"But where's Jenny?"

"Jenny!" I called.

There was still no response.

"JENNY!"

"Here I am," she said cheerily, her head emerging from under a pile of books.

"Shush in there!" said Mr. Shush's voice from somewhere above us.

"Mr. Shush!" yelled Newton. "Help us! Please! We're trapped!"

"Shush!" said Mr. Shush.

"But we're trapped!"

"I'm well aware of that," said Mr. Shush. "Penny and Gina rode Jack into the end shelf and knocked it over. It created a domino effect, the unfortunate result of which is that eight shelves of books are now completely out of order."

"Not to mention that *we're trapped*!" said Gretel.

"All right. All right!" said Mr. Shush. "Calm down. And be quiet. I'm working on getting you out."

"Well, what's taking so long?" I asked.

"Well, I can't just remove the books willy-nilly," said Mr. Shush. "I have to do it systematically. In alphabetical order. This is a library, you know, not a garage sale."

Chapter 58

Minutes . . .

The seconds turned into minutes. . . .

Chapter 59

Hours . . .

. . . The minutes turned into hours. . . .

Chapter 60

Days . . .

. . . The hours turned into days. . . .

Chapter 61

Weeks . . .

. . . The days turned into weeks. . . .

Chapter 62

Months . . .

. . . The weeks turned into months. . . .

Chapter 63

Years . . .

. . . The months turned into years. . . .

Well, it probably didn't take quite *that* long for Mr. Shush to remove the books alphabetically and stack them in neat little piles, but it sure felt like it.

Chapter 64

Rescue

"Do you think we'll ever get out?" asked Newton.

"Yes," I said, "of course we will!"

"But what if we don't?" he said. "What if we're trapped here forever? What will we eat? What if we have to eat each other? That will make us cannibals. I don't want to be a cannibal. I'm scared of cannibals!"

"Snap out of it, Newton!" said Gretel. "You're getting hysterical!"

"Yes, calm down, Newton." Jenny's voice was more calm. "You don't have to be a cannibal if you don't want to be. None of us do."

"But what are we going to eat?" said Newton. "Books?"

"There'll be no book-eating in my library!" cried Mr. Shush, as he finally removed the books that were blocking the end of the row. Our crawl space flooded with light.

We could see Mr. Shush, Fred, Clive, Gina, Penny, and Jack peering in at us.

"Hallelujah!" I yelled. "We're saved!"

"Shush!" said Mr. Shush. "Keep it down! This is a *library*, you know, not a church!"

Chapter 65

Liftoff!

After Mr. Shush had slowly and methodically removed as many of the books as possible, he was — with Gina, Penny, and Jack's help — finally able to lift the shelf off of us.

Fred and Clive, who couldn't help with the shelf because of their injuries, tried hard to hide their disappointment that we were relatively injury-free.

In fact, the only one of us who seemed to have sustained any injury at all was Jack, who was rubbing his head and looking confused.

"Are you all right, Henry?" he asked.

"You've got your memory back!" I said. "That's great!"

"A book fell on his head," said Gina, "when he bumped into the shelf."

"Yeah, poor Ponyboy," said Penny, stroking Jack's hair.

Jack pulled his head away and gave her a dirty look. "Quit it!" he warned.

"What's the matter, Jack?" said Gina. "Don't you want to play ponies anymore?"

"No!" said Jack, looking horrified. "As if!"

Gina and Penny looked sadly at each other.

Fred and Clive smirked.

As Gretel, Newton, and I stood up and climbed out over the books that we'd been lying on, I saw the pencil on the carpet.

Only it wasn't a pencil anymore.

It was just a pile of crushed splinters. It had been completely shattered by the weight of the falling bookshelf. There was nothing left of the eraser, either. It was just a little pile of white dust.

"Look," I said to the others. "It couldn't be buried, disposed of, crushed, or compacted. But the one power that it was powerless against was its own."

"Yeah," said Gretel. "It drew its own doom."

"Poor pencil," said Jenny, shaking her head. "If only it could have used its power for good instead of evil."

I put my hand on Newton's shoulder. "You can stop worrying now," I said. "The nightmare is over."

"I'll never stop worrying," said Newton, smiling weakly. "But at least I have one less thing to worry about."

Jack rolled his eyes. "I don't believe you guys," he said. "It was just a *coincidence*. It was just *bad luck* that the shelves fell over and the pencil got squashed. That pencil was not *evil. It was the best pencil ever. And now it's wrecked!*"

"SHUSH!" yelled Mr. Shush. "STOP YELLING! MAY I REMIND YOU THAT THIS IS A LIBRARY?!"

Chapter 66

Mr. Brainfright's magic hat

The following morning, Mr. Brainfright came into class dressed in a top hat and tails and carrying a shiny black cane.

"Okay, everyone, please take your seats," he said. "The show is about to begin."

We all rushed to our seats.

The bell rang.

Mr. Brainfright took off his tall black top hat and sat it upside down on his desk. Then he tapped the brim of the hat twice with his cane and said, "Abracadabra."

Then he reached into the hat and pulled out a fluffy white rabbit. A *real, live* fluffy white rabbit.

"Oh, it's so *cute*!" said Jenny.

We all applauded.

Mr. Brainfright put the rabbit back in the hat, tapped the brim twice again, and turned the hat right side up. The rabbit was gone.

"Oh," said Jenny, "bring it back! Pleeeeeease!"

Mr. Brainfright put the hat back on the desk, upside down, said, "Abracadabra!" as he tapped the brim with his cane, and pulled the rabbit out once more.

"What's the matter, Newton?" asked Jenny.

I looked over. As usual, Newton was looking pale and wide-eyed.

"I'm scared of magic rabbits," he said.

"There's no need to be frightened," Mr. Brainfright assured him. "The rabbit is not *magic*. I am simply demonstrating what is known as 'sleight of hand.' It's a perfectly ordinary rabbit, I assure you."

"It's not ordinary," said Jenny. "It's *adorable*. Can I hold it, Mr. Brainfright, please?"

"Of course," he said, taking it over to her desk and putting it in her arms.

"See?" Jenny said to Newton as she cuddled the rabbit. "It's completely cute and harmless."

Newton leaned over and tentatively patted the rabbit.

"It's soft," he said.

"Yes, and think of it this way, Newton," said Mr. Brainfright. "It has four rabbit's feet, so it's four times as lucky as your one."

Newton smiled at this happy thought and patted the rabbit more boldly.

"And speaking of rabbit's feet, may I use this to demonstrate my next illusion?" said Mr. Brainfright as he picked up Newton's lucky rabbit's foot off his desk.

Newton made a grab for it but was too slow. "I'm not sure about this, sir," he said. "Can't you use something else?"

"No, this will be perfect," said Mr. Brainfright. "And don't worry — I'm only going to borrow it for a moment. You'll get it back."

He picked his top hat up off the desk and dropped the rabbit's foot into it. He said, "Abracadabra," tapped the brim of the hat twice with his shiny black cane, and then tipped the hat right side up.

The rabbit's foot did not drop out.

It was gone!

Everyone in the class clapped — except Newton.

Then Mr. Brainfright tapped his cane twice on the brim of the hat and said, "Abracadabra."

But the foot didn't come back. Which is what I assumed was supposed to happen because Mr. Brainfright looked very surprised and then confused. He looked into the hat.

Newton gasped in alarm. "My rabbit's foot," he squeaked.

Mr. Brainfright frowned into the hat. "Don't worry, Newton," he said. "It's in there. It's just stuck . . . I think."

"But what if you can't find it?" said Newton. "I'll never have good luck again!"

"Pat the rabbit some more," Jenny said to Newton, putting it into his arms. "It's very soothing."

Newton stared at Mr. Brainfright's top hat and patted the rabbit automatically.

He didn't look soothed.

Meanwhile, Mr. Brainfright just kept tapping his hat with his cane and trying different spells. "Abracadabra . . . sim sala bim . . . bibbitdily bobbitdily boo . . ." But still the rabbit's foot did not appear.

"Perhaps if I put the rabbit back in it might help unstick the foot," said Mr. Brainfright, reaching for the rabbit.

Newton pulled it closer against his chest. "No," he said. "You can't have it. What if you can't get it out again?"

"No, don't make it disappear," said Jenny. "Let us keep it. Can we have it for a class pet? Please, Mr. Brainfright, please?"

"I'm sure it would bring us good luck, sir," said Newton. "Like you said — it's got four rabbit's feet, and that's four times luckier than one."

Mr. Brainfright looked down at their pleading faces.

"Well, all right," he finally said. "We'll get a hutch for it and it can be the class pet."

"Thank you, Mr. Brainfright," said Jenny.

"Can we get a pony as well?" asked Gina.

"Yes," said Penny. "Can you make one come out of your hat?"

"No, I think my hat's finished for the day," said Mr. Brainfright, peering into it with a puzzled expression on his face.

"Awwwwww," said the twins.

"Sorry," said Mr. Brainfright, "but sometimes these magic hats have minds of their own."

Fiona duly noted this fact down.

"Will we be tested on this?" she asked.

Chapter 67

Mr. Brainfright's important lesson no. 5

Sometimes magic hats have minds of their own.

Chapter 68

The last chapter

Well, that's my story.

And just in case you're wondering, it's all true.

Every last bit.

If you're ever passing through Northwest, and you happen to be passing Northwest Southeast Central School, feel free to drop in.

We're pretty easy to find. Our classroom is the first on the left as you go up the steps.

And our teacher wears a purple jacket.

But don't forget to stop by the office first and sign the visitors' book.

And don't waste time while you're doing it. As I think I have mentioned, Mrs. Rosethorn doesn't like time-wasters.

Anyway, it would be great to see you, and if you enjoyed this story, then don't worry, I've got plenty more!

And they're all true.

Every last one.